IN THE DISMAL SWAMP

IN THE DISMAL SWAMP

•

Patrick Balester

AVALON BOOKS
NEW YORK

Published by Thomas Bouregy & Co., Inc.
160 Madison Avenue, New York, NY 10016

Library of Congress Cataloging-in-Publication Data

Balester, Patrick.
In the Dismal Swamp / Patrick Balester.
     p.   cm.
ISBN 978-0-8034-9899-0 (acid-free paper)
   1. Politicians' spouses—Crimes against—Fiction.
2. Murder—Investigation—Fiction.   3. Dismal Swamp
(N.C. and Va.)—Fiction.   I. Title.

PS3602.A59548I65 2008
813'.6—dc22   2007047386

PRINTED IN THE UNITED STATES OF AMERICA
ON ACID-FREE PAPER
BY HADDON CRAFTSMEN, BLOOMSBURG, PENNSYLVANIA

To my loving wife,
who is never far from my thoughts
when I am contemplating murder.

Many people assisted in the creation of this story. I would like to acknowledge the assistance of the men and women of the US Fish and Wildlife Service, who answered many of my questions about the Great Dismal Swamp Wildlife Refuge.

Also, I wish to thank my editor, Faith Black, whose editing skills were not only priceless, but also painless.

Chapter One

A single thread of smoke rose in the clearing where the three men sat around a dying campfire. One threw small bits of kindling into the embers and watched them smoke and then burst into flame. With each flare, he smiled and waited until the twig turned to red embers before he threw in another. A second man sat on a split log; his head bobbed up and down, then jerked as he tried to fend off sleep. The third, pig-faced and more restless than the others, stared into the woods around them. His thick chin jutted beneath his frowning thin lips. Dawn was a half hour away.

"Where the devil is he?" he asked no one in particular. He stood and paced around the fire. Leaves and stone crunched under his boots. Again he peered into the woods, rubbed his snout, paced some more, and sat

1

down on a rock. He sat for only a minute before he stood and repeated the process.

"Take a load off," the sleepy one said. "He'll get here when he gets here."

"Shut up!" the pacer ordered. "He was supposed to be here an hour ago. We've got to be out of here by dawn. I don't plan on getting caught in the open. Clean this place up!" he exclaimed, and he kicked at an open sleeping bag. Next he aimed for one of the pup tents that sagged in the gray morning. Fog hung low among the conifers above them, and a thin layer of dew clung to the canvas.

A snapping sound caught the men's attention, and all three turned toward the source. The pacer reached behind his waist and rested his thumb on the back of a Beretta 9-mm. The contact with the steel steadied his nerves.

"Greg?" he called.

There was no reply. He was about to call out again, when a voice interceded.

"Fish and Wildlife! Drop your weapons, and put your hands up!" the disembodied voice ordered. In the early-morning mist, it sounded faraway and lonely, but it got the men's attention. All three stood up, the sleepy one almost tottering over as he wrestled with consciousness.

"We're just camping here. We're unarmed," the pacer called out after a moment's indecision.

"Just the same, keep your hands where I can see them," the voice commanded. Another branch cracked in the woods, and a masculine form took shape at the edge of the clearing and slowly marched toward them.

The pacer could see the intruder clearly now—tall and

wearing jeans and a hooded red sweatshirt—and he motioned the others, who had crowded around him and into his line of sight, away with short, furious movements of his left hand. The right hand still rested on his Beretta, and he faced the approaching form squarely to hide this fact. A few more steps and he would have a dead-on shot to the man's chest. A small trickle of sweat ran down the back of his neck, and goose bumps dotted his arms beneath his heavy flannel shirt. He tightened his grip, placed his index finger in the trigger guard, and whipped the gun around to his front. One of the men screamed. Before he could focus the gun's sight on the approaching man's chest, he froze and then let his arm go limp. The gun dangled from his thumb and forefinger.

"Greg!"

"What d'ya know!"

Greg pulled back his hood as he stepped into the makeshift camp and grinned. "Hey, Buckles. How's it hanging?" he asked, as though he had just arrived for a barbecue.

" 'How's it hangin'?' I'll tell you how it's 'hangin'.' You almost got shot, my friend. That's how it's hangin'," the pig-faced man said, and he pushed the Beretta back into the waist of his dungarees.

"What d'ya know!" the fire feeder repeated.

"Hey, Greg. Where you been?" the sleepy one, now fully awake, asked.

"Thought I'd stir up a little excitement for you. Didn't want you getting bored," Greg teased.

But Buckles would not be mollified. He kept the

same stern face on and pulled away from Greg, who towered over him by almost a foot. "You're lucky, that's all," Buckles said, and he continued to pout.

The others sat down around the fire, and Greg pulled off his pack and opened it to reveal a bag of Krispy Kreme donuts. As the men cheered with voices loud and rude, Greg shook the bag at Buckles with a smile.

Buckles continued to frown even as he paced his way over to the group and grabbed the bag from Greg. "Gimme that!" he roared. Finally he sat. "Don't do that again," he ordered. He picked two of the fattest donuts and tossed the bag at his compatriots, who scrambled for the doughy treats. Greg simply sat and watched.

"Hey, Greg, want one?" Sleepy mumbled, and he stuffed his second donut into his cheeks.

Before Greg could respond, Buckles intervened. "No donuts for him!" he complained. "Your penalty," he added, glaring at Greg.

"Hey, I already had mine," Greg said, and he threw out his arms nonchalantly. He sat and watched the others eat with barely concealed delight. Only Buckles continued to make faces, and that only when he caught Greg looking in his direction. As they licked the last of the sugar from their fingers, Greg stood up and stretched. "How about some coffee? Then we can talk business."

"Now that Greg's here, can we split the stash?" the fire starter asked.

"After coffee, we split it and then split up. After today," Buckles added with emphasis, "we don't call each other again. Agreed?" He embraced the circle with his eyes. Each man nodded in assent.

Buckles looked around, then pulled a coffeepot from a pile of clothes and camping gear and tossed it at the sleeper.

"Hurry up! No, you idiot, the stream is that way!" he said, pointing behind the still-dazed man, who ambled down the hill toward the creek below the camp.

Only then did Buckles begin to relax. "Well, I must say, this has been a lot of fun, boys," he said, and he finally smiled. "I hate to end this beautiful relationship, but—"

"Buckles!" a voice called from the stream. A moment later they heard, "US Fish and Wildlife police! Put your hands up!"

For a moment, Buckles tensed, and the fire starter pointed at his leader and laughed. "Ha-ha. He got ya that time!"

Greg shook his head and buried it in his folded arms, but his heaving shoulders gave him away.

Buckles swore and stood. Cupping his hands together, he called down to the stream, "Bert! That's not funny!" A moment of silence was followed by Bert's voice again, but this time all three men stood and cocked their ears toward the sound.

There were now two voices coming from the creek below the camp, and in the woods snapping twigs and more voices erupted.

"Fish and Wildlife police! You three around the fire, stand still. Don't move!"

"What do we do?" the fire starter asked, unsure of which way to turn.

But Buckles was already running in the opposite direction of the voices, with Greg tight on his heels. "Run, you fools!" Buckles called back over his shoulder, then added, "And if you get caught, you don't know me!" His short legs moved faster than seemed possible as he dove into the woods in a panic.

A voice called out from the front and right of him. He paused, looking for a way out amid the underbrush. Shots rang out behind him, and he flinched and ducked. He turned to see Greg firing three shots in rapid succession toward the voice that had called out to them. Buckles could just make out a figure behind a tree seventy-five yards ahead.

Greg grabbed his arm and pulled him to the left. "This way!" he yelled, and the two men scrambled down a steep incline and deeper into the forest.

Behind them, the officer Greg had pinned down spoke into a radio. "Shots fired. I need backup!" the voice said.

Greg and Buckles scrambled to hold their footing until the ground leveled out. Buckles swung his arms wildly to balance his charging weight, which he could not slow, and he nearly ran into Greg, who turned and opened his arms to catch him, sending them both to the pine-needle–covered forest floor. The soft bedding was the only thing that allowed them to stand again without broken bones. The tangle of waving limbs and several choice words from Buckles startled a raccoon, which swiftly disappeared into the underbrush.

"What are you doing?" Buckles hissed. "Firing at a cop! Are you nuts?"

"Relax!" Greg said. "I fired above him. Anyway, we got away, didn't we?"

At that, both men looked around and listened. Buckles moved back-to-back with Greg, and they revolved in a circle before they were satisfied.

"C'mon. My truck's just a few hundred yards away," Greg said, and he headed farther into the woods. He stopped when Buckles refused to move. "What's the matter?" he asked.

Buckles was rubbing his chin. Then he looked at Greg, as if appraising a job candidate at an interview. He stared hard at the man.

Greg repeated his question. "What's wrong? We've got to go!"

"The stash," he finally said quietly.

"What?" Greg threw up his arms. "Forget that, man! We can't go back there. We're toast if we get found in these woods. I've got clothes and fishing poles in the truck. Let's go!"

"No," Buckles insisted. "Look, I'll cut you in for half. We don't need Tommy and Bert anymore."

"Half? What good does half do me in jail?" Greg countered. "Man, I'm out of here." And he turned away.

"No, wait! Look, Greg, I got a dozen dried gallbladders, almost fifty paws, and skins! I got skins we can sell for hundreds apiece! Do you know what one skin goes for in LA? Almost a thousand!"

"So what? The stash is nowhere near here," Greg argued. "It's back the way we came!"

"No, it's not," Buckles said simply. "It's less than a mile away."

Greg's eyes hardened.

"Yeah, I know. I lied. So shoot me," Buckles conceded.

"But how—" Greg began.

"Shh!" Buckles commanded. He brought out his compass and found north. With a stubby finger he pointed twenty degrees north-northwest. He looked up and toward his destination. "That way." He took off at a trot and waved Greg forward. Greg followed more slowly and continued to shake his head. The men picked up the pace after a few minutes. Buckles stopped twice to take another compass reading. The third time he stopped, he was panting.

"I gotta rest," he panted, and he leaned bent at the waist, his hands on his thighs.

"Uh, I think we should keep moving," Greg intervened.

"For Chrissakes!" Buckles said, and then he froze as a noise reached his ears. Greg was already listening to the faint but definite sound of baying dogs.

"Like I said . . ."

"Right."

The sound gave new energy to their legs, Greg's lean and long, Buckles' short and stocky. They ran for several more minutes, and then Buckles clapped.

"There! That's the boulder I was looking for." He ran into a cove formed by a semicircle of rocks. The center was covered with poison oak and blackberry bushes. The razor-sharp thorns bit into Greg, who halted at the edge. Buckles dove in, pushing aside the brambles with barely a word of complaint.

"Don't you see it?" he asked, beaming proudly.

"See what? I just see a bunch of thorns and bushes," Greg complained as he followed Buckles gingerly to the center of the semicircle.

"That's 'cause you're not looking in the right place," he said, and with that he stamped on the ground, which gave a hollow sound.

Before Greg's startled mind could pour out questions, Buckles pulled on a pair of leather gloves from his coat and pulled back the shrubs and tangled vines. Beneath them, moss-covered and smelling of earth, was a wooden door. Both men listened for another moment and then bent down to lift it. The door swung open on rusty, creaking hinges.

Greg pulled out a flashlight. "But how? How'd you make this?" he asked in astonishment.

"I didn't," Buckles replied. "It's an old root cellar. When I was a kid, an old lady lived here. We used to pick strawberries in her garden, run errands—the usual stuff. Her house was decrepit even then, and when she died, they tore it down. But they left the root cellar," he said excitedly.

As they looked in, the smell of fur and skin drifted up to them. They stepped down three damp, slippery steps into the musky cellar. Greg surveyed the trophies illuminated by the swaying circle of light. The walls were covered with bear and deer skins. Several sets of antlers hung above them and in a knotted pile in a corner. Shelves held jars containing alcohol and paws cut from the limbs of poached black bears. One large jar, to Greg's dismay, held the body of an infant cub, probably no more than a week old. The paws of the mother were probably among the grisly collection. The smell was stronger now, like that of an animal's den, but mixed with the sickly, pungent odor of guts and blood that made both men cough.

"After a while, there was no one around who even remembered that a house had ever stood here. But I didn't forget," Buckles said. He pointed. "Help me with the cooler." A ten-gallon Coleman stood against the earthen wall to their left, and with a man at each handle, they dragged and pushed it up the steps and into the light. They lifted the heavy door and gently placed it back over the entrance. Once done, they rested for a moment, both of them breathing deeply. Buckles wiped his face with a shirtsleeve.

"We'll come back for the rest later, when the heat's off. In the meantime"—he patted the cooler—"we can hide out on the money we get from this."

"The gallbladders?" Greg asked.

Buckles nodded. "We can get four, maybe five thousand for them, easy." Buckles perked up, and both of them listened for the faint sound of dogs, but only buzzing insects and birdsong greeted their ears.

"Help me cover this back up," Buckles said as he stood. He pushed and grabbed the vines, moving them over the cellar. He fussed like a maid doing housework while Greg feigned his efforts. "Never mind," Buckles said. "Let me do it. It has to look natural!" Greg stepped back and let Buckles work. He placed the finishing touches on his handiwork, then, hands on his hips, stepped back and surveyed the ground.

"There. No one will find this unless they fall into it," he announced as he removed his gloves. "Well, looks like we're done here."

"You don't know the half of it," Greg's voice said from behind him.

Buckles turned, gloves still in hand, and found the barrel of a gun pointed right at him. "What the—? You backstabber!" He stepped forward, and Greg raised his aim. That brought Buckles to a halt, but his mouth went on.

"After I trusted you! You think you can steal from me? You'll never get those parts sold without me!" he bellowed, even as his hands went up in response to Greg's gestures with the gun.

"Uh, I wasn't thinking of selling them," Greg replied, and he pulled his wallet out and flipped it open to reveal a gold badge. "US Fish and Wildlife. You're under arrest. On your knees!" Greg ordered.

Buckles' jaw dropped open, and his eyes widened in astonishment. His shoulders slumped, and he suddenly seemed smaller, as though his abdomen was a balloon with a slow but steady leak. He was speechless as Greg secured handcuffs on him, read him his rights, and spoke to someone on a walkie-talkie he removed from its hiding place under one pant leg.

"Yeah, I got him. Led me right to his hidden cache. Looks like Operation Soup is now officially over," Greg said, referring to the undercover sting that had broken up the largest poaching gang in the Smoky Mountain Forest. A muffled reply, unintelligible to Buckles but heard by Greg, prompted a reply. "No, we'll rest a minute here, and I'll walk him in." Greg surveyed the tree canopy overhead. "We don't need a chopper. No room to land, and you've got the GPS. Send someone out to get the stuff."

He sat down on a rock across from Buckles, who still knelt, his head dipped and resting on his chest.

"Buckles, Buckles."

Slowly, Buckles looked up. Greg was smiling.

"What are you grinnin' at, you hick?" Buckles growled. His astonishment forgotten, he struggled briefly against his restraints. He tried to stand, but without the use of his arms, he couldn't.

"I was just thinking," Greg continued, "about when you started running, at the camp. Man, I can still picture those short little legs of yours moving a hundred miles an hour. And when you looked back, without even slowing down, and yelled, 'You don't know me'— remember?"

Buckles didn't reply, but his lips moved and spittle formed at the edges of his grimace.

"Man, I almost gave it up, right then and there." Greg chuckled. "I nearly burst out laughing and blew my cover. Do you really think Tommy and Bert will keep quiet? Those guys are singing right now." Greg laughed again as Buckles let loose a stream of obscenities that echoed through the forest.

Chapter Two

Five thousand years ago, in a lonely spot three dozen miles west of the Virginia Beach coastline, the local Indian tribes claim that a great fire bird fell from the sky and burned a deep hole into the earth. From this scar emerged what the white settlers of early Virginia called Lake Drummond. Besides being the largest natural lake in Virginia, it is the crown jewel at the center of a wide swath of wilderness that desperate men and frightened children know only as the Great Dismal Swamp.

For uncounted generations, only wandering bands of Indians used it as a favored hunting ground. After the appearance of settlers from England, the Nansemond tribe abandoned the swamp. Its unexplored paths were avoided by the Europeans, who saw it as a harbor for disease, hunger, and ghostly spirits.

From Colonial times until the end of the American

Civil War, it became a refuge for runaway slaves, who used its impenetrable depths to hide from local vigilantes. No respectable man would allow his hunting dogs to enter the impassable depths of the dark swamp. Those who did so soon lost the scent among the bogs and trunks of bald cypress and Atlantic white cedar trees that dominated the landscape.

Indeed, the trees were a major source of income for George Washington, who purchased four thousand acres of the Great Dismal Swamp after leaving the presidency. His plans to drain the swamp and convert it to a rice plantation failed. But timber and cypress shingles became a profitable venture, and a road, named for our first president and which exists even today, was built from the western edge of the swamp to Lake Drummond. Its name, the Washington Ditch, fails to convey its value as a highway for bird-watchers, hikers, bicyclists, and other tourists, as well as the occasional deer seen feeding at the side of the road between the gravel bed and the dark waters of the adjacent canal.

The Washington Ditch is accessed by driving down poorly marked country roads in Suffolk, Virginia, but a patient traveler is well rewarded if he or she ventures down that tree-lined trail for four or five miles, because at the end of it lies Lake Drummond. The prehistoric waters of this isolated lake have charmed and awed settlers for hundreds of years. For those adventurous souls whose spirit is willing but whose flesh, or the lack of a good pair of hiking boots, prevents them from making the ten-mile round-trip the eastern side of the swamp permits access by boat at a boat ramp off Route 17. The canal, known as the Feeder Ditch, can take you to the lake in just a couple of hours by canoe, less by motor-boat.

A slow trip by water into the middle of the Great Dismal Swamp is like no other adventure you will ever take. The natural beauty and peace of the place will make you forget that men and women once struggled and fought and died to tame this impenetrable wilder-ness and, to this day, sometimes still surrender their souls under cover of night when the moon is hidden and the furry and amphibious witnesses are mute.

Not far from the lake, in a small diner in the neigh-boring town of Great Bridge, sat a man by the name of Floyd Culpepper, wearing a uniform of the National Wildlife Refuge Police. The Great Dismal Swamp was his territory. He guarded it and loved it. He drank a cup of coffee and occasionally glanced out the front window.

"Not quite yet, thank you," he muttered to the inquir-ing waitress. "I'm waiting for someone."

A dusty-looking Toyota Corolla pulled up to The Grill, and a tall, lanky youth got out and headed for the door. He might have been confused for a cook or bus-boy or a high school kid looking for a job, if not for the same uniform worn by Floyd Culpepper, the pant creases neatly pressed and a tie snugly around the neck. But there the resemblance ended. This boy had a crew cut that made his thin features even more pronounced, and an egg-shaped head with the point ending in a chin that sat atop a long, thin neck broken only by an Adam's apple that bobbed when he spoke. Combined with long arms and large hands, the effect was almost comical, except for the uniform. And the gun, of course. Not the same model gun that Floyd carried, but the same authority that allowed him to carry it, and beneath the sharp, pressed shirt, the heart of a man who wasn't afraid to draw it, if need be.

On this particular morning, there wasn't a need to draw a weapon, but the man hesitated at the door and then opened it slowly, as though he was prepared to confront a poacher rather than meet his new boss. It was the latter that accounted for his nervousness. After a moment's hesitation, he opened the door and went in. He spotted Floyd, joined him at the table, and shook his hand. Before he spoke, the waitress brought a cup and filled it with regular.

"So, we finally meet," Floyd began. "Have any trouble with traffic?"

"Not in this town," Greg said with a smile. "I made it from home in about ten minutes."

"Well, I've got a bit more of a drive, since I live in Suffolk on the other side of the swamp. Got an old farmhouse I'm fixing up. Did you want to order?" Floyd asked and glanced up at the counter, where the waitress stood by a hot plate.

"I'll have eggs, over easy, hash browns, and toast," Greg replied. He glanced at Floyd expectantly.

"Oh, they know me here—pancakes, eggs, and sausage for me," he said.

"Be right up," a voice called from the counter.

"Well, let me tell you a little about our team here, and then you can tell me something about Operation Soup. I understand you made quite a name for yourself on that one last year," Floyd remarked, and he noticed the pride in Greg's face, despite his attempt to hide it. "We operate on a shoestring budget, unfortunately. The state doesn't part with a penny unless it has to, and most of the Federal budget for the refuge system goes out west, or farther south to the better-known refuges. We don't have any grizzlies or wolves or elk, the big-name animals that draw people, so, naturally, we suffer for it. But we manage to get a lot done. In fact, we recently added about five thousand acres in the northeast corner that need to be marked, and that's one of the tasks I'd like to get you started on. Are you familiar with the swamp, been in it much?"

"Not lately, but when I was a kid, I traveled here every summer. And I've been studying the maps you mailed me, and the major features." Greg looked up, and a plate was placed before him. He took a bite before glancing at Floyd, who continued.

"Okay, well, you'll get your feet wet soon enough, and I mean that. Waterproof boots are a must in this line of work. Anyway, the main long-term goal we have here is to repopulate the refuge with Atlantic white cedar and cypress gum trees. They used to make up the major vegetation here, but years of logging and road building has—" Here he paused and raised his hands together, resting the fingertips under his chin. A pained expression crossed his face as the thought formed in his head. "Well, the natural flow of water, the hydrology of the swamp, has been destroyed, and red maple has begun to take over the drier areas. White cedar is pretty rare except in the southern parts, which are wetter, and, of course, cypress was the main tree harvested here. I'm grateful to Union Camp for donating most of the land that makes up the refuge, but they sure took everything out of her that they could before giving her to us."

"So, you need to change that?"

"We've been planting cedar and cypress, and we want to, over time, restore the swamp to its natural state. And to keep the water from stagnating in those spots behind the old logging roads, we're using water gates and ditches to restore flow. This takes years, of course. I've been here fifteen, and it'll take another fifteen to thirty years to see significant changes, but . . . we'll get there." Floyd leaned back. He paused for a moment while Greg attacked his food. His young, darting movements were silent yet determined, and with each stab, the fork tines found their mark.

"Maybe I'll get to see the job finished," Greg said after swallowing.

"I hope to see it too, though I'll be retired by then. But you may get to have a hand in finishing it, assuming you want to stay. After the success of your last assignment, you could have picked any refuge in the country. Is this place enough of a challenge for you?" Floyd inquired.

"You could make a career here, although I imagine a young buck like you would like to move on eventually, do something more exciting."

"Nah," Greg replied. "My mom lives in Great Bridge, and she's got arthritis really bad. I kinda like to be nearby in case she needs help. Been staying with her while I look for a place."

The two men finished their breakfast and received coffee refills.

"Now, why don't you tell me what you're looking for in this position?" Floyd asked. "It may not be as exciting as catching armed poachers," he remarked, referring to Greg's last assignment as an undercover mole in Operation Soup.

"Oh, yeah. That was a lot of fun!" Greg said.

"I understand you infiltrated the group. How'd you manage that?" Floyd asked.

Greg thought for a moment, gazing at his coffee cup. "A lot of people say I look younger than I really am," he began, "and when I want to, I can act pretty immature."

"Sort of like just 'acting your age'?" Floyd inquired.

"Pretty much," Greg said with a laugh. "You've got the idea. So I let myself get spotted 'poaching' by the ringleader in the Smoky Mountain Forest, fully armed and loaded for bear, so to speak. I acted as if I'd been caught with my hand in the cookie jar, just some local hick out to bag himself a trophy. I even asked him if he was a cop while we chatted, acting really nervous. Well, he bought it, and then he asked if I wanted to go to a target range—his idea. I knew what he wanted—to see if I could shoot with any accuracy. Of course, being a marksman from my military service helped with that. I tried to play it down, but he got pretty excited. At a bar that night, he and a couple of his buddies approached me about making some real money selling bear parts. I pretended I'd never heard of the Asian market, and when he said I could get a hundred dollars for just one bear paw, I told him he was nuts—still playing the hick. I actually told him I'd have to think about it," Greg said slowly. "Well, after a few more phone calls and drinks at the bar, I agreed to come on board."

"How did you discover his hidden stash?" Floyd asked.

"Now *that* required some thought," Greg said. "We knew he had a large number of parts, including at least a dozen gallbladders."

"The source of the bile," Floyd added.

"Exactly."

"Ewww! What is that?" a voice interrupted. The waitress paused in midstride as she moved between the tables.

"Do you want to take this?" Floyd smiled and motioned to Greg.

"It's a fluid that comes from the bear's gallbladder. Asians use it in their traditional medicine," Greg explained. "It's supposedly an aphrodisiac, and many men use it to enhance their, shall we say, stamina," he said innocently.

"Bile?" the waitress exclaimed. Her shoulders shivered, which caused the coffee in her carafe to slosh back and forth before she turned away. She tossed up a hand to signal her disgust. An old man at the counter laughed at her facial expression as she refilled his cup. She shivered each time she repeated the word.

Greg leaned a little closer to the table as he took another sip of coffee and then whispered to Floyd, "I love to tell that story." Floyd chuckled and pushed his plate back from the edge of the table.

"So, you were saying," Floyd began.

"Oh, yeah. So, we planned a raid, even though we didn't know where his stash was hidden. But he was greedy—I knew he'd never leave it behind," Greg said grimly. "Those kind are all alike." For a moment Greg was lost in thought, and it was only when he caught the eyes of his future boss that he abruptly continued. "I arranged for us to 'escape' the raid and offered to help get him away in my truck. True to form, he wouldn't go without his stash. He led me right to it, in an old, abandoned root cellar of some house that was torn down years ago. You should have seen the look on his face when he emerged from the cellar, turned around, and found me pointing a gun at him with one hand, my badge in the other."

"I'll bet he was surprised."

Greg could only smile in response.

"How was everything?" the waitress asked. At their affirmative nods, she smiled and added, "If you need anything else, you just let me know," and she placed the check facedown between them.

Floyd picked up the check, glanced at his watch, and

pushed his chair back. Greg took the cue, and both men headed for the door.

"Thanks, come again," the owner called out, poised before the hot griddle, where he nursed a pile of hash browns.

Floyd paid the bill, and Greg looked back at their waitress as she cleared the table. As she looked up, he gave a small nod, and she smiled.

"You come back soon, now, you hear?" she ordered with a broad smile. Her brown eyes glittered.

"Yes, ma'am," he replied, saluting.

"Amanda," she confided.

"Greg Parnell. Nice to meet you."

"Likewise," she said, and she turned her attention to the next customer looking for a refill on his coffee. Her brown locks swayed sensuously above her shoulders.

Once outside, Greg shook hands with Floyd.

"See you Monday at the office. You know where it is, don't you?" Floyd asked.

Greg nodded, and he watched Floyd's pickup pull out of the lot before he headed to his car.

Chapter Three

The weekend came and went, and on Monday the alarm woke Greg at six in the morning. After a leisurely breakfast at The Grill and some friendly chat with Amanda, he drove the twenty minutes to the National Wildlife Refuge headquarters. He waited in the parking lot until he saw lights coming on in the one-story building. He recognized Floyd's pickup, and a Ford Escort stood next to it. In the opposite corner of the parking lot sat another pickup, this one emblazoned on the side with the logo of the Fish & Wildlife Service. He turned off the ignition and reached for the door handle.

God, I hope I don't get bored. With that thought, he opened the car door and stepped out. *Only 7,200 days until retirement.*

He walked through the door at 8:30 A.M. and was greeted by the wide smile of a woman who strode out from behind a counter to meet him. She extended a hand, which he took.

"Hi, you must be Greg!" she smiled. "I'm Cindy. Welcome to the Great Dismal Swamp."

"Thanks. I guess you were expecting me," he replied.

"Floyd told us all about you," she said. "And, speak of the devil, here he is."

Floyd emerged from his office. "Well, you remembered how to get here?" he asked as he shook Greg's hand.

"Oh, you've been here before?" Cindy inquired.

"We used to vacation at Virginia Beach when I was a kid. My mom liked the sand, but Dad always took me at least once into the Dismal Swamp. Our first trip in, we went to Lake Drummond in a canoe along the Feeder Ditch. I've been hooked on this place ever since."

"Well, it is beautiful, that's for sure. Might not be too exciting for you, though. It's not too late to change your mind," Floyd warned with a smile.

"Oh, no!" Cindy said. "I've already processed his paperwork. He's staying!"

"Well, all right then. Let me show you around the place. Most of the crew is out in the field. You'll meet them later. In the meantime, I'll give you the rundown on our little operation. We've had some reports of a man collecting rare butterflies illegally, but we haven't turned up anything definite. Still, it might give you something to do while I'm gone."

"You're leaving?" Greg said, surprised.

"Oh, that's right, you wouldn't know. It's my mother.

She's in the hospital in Florida, so I'll be gone for a week or so. She's had cancer for a long time, and she's eighty, so I've been expecting this for a while," Floyd explained.

"I'm sorry to hear that," Greg said softly. He thought of his own mother and quietly understood the need to leave to be by her side.

"Thanks. But for today, at least, we'll get you all situated. Anything you need, just ask Cindy. Let's look around and see if you have any questions," Floyd offered.

"Okay."

For the next several hours, Greg got a tour of the facility, reviewed the current projects being performed, and analyzed a map of the refuge with Floyd. As other members of the staff wandered in, he got to meet them and hear their jokes and their version of what kind of boss Floyd would make. Everyone was pleasant and offered to assist him.

By the time Greg got into his car that night, he was feeling at home. And with Floyd being gone for a few days, he could settle in and explore the swamp at his own pace. He was still trying to keep all the trail names and their locations straight in his head. A small laminated map that Floyd gave him was small enough to slip into his shirt pocket, and he took it home to study over dinner.

The thought of a hot meal tempted him to pick up speed along Route 337 in Suffolk, but the winding road was not cooperating. Only after he crossed the Norfolk southern railroad tracks and turned right onto Highway 13 could he accelerate. He merged into Interstate 64 and got off two exits later to Great Bridge, traveling south along Battlefield Boulevard. At the Great Bridge Shopping Center, he turned right onto Johnstown Road and passed new construction of two- and three-story luxury homes that were beginning to spring up in Great Bridge.

He soon pulled into the driveway of a ranch-style cinder-block house, whitewashed, with a small dogwood in the front lawn by the door. In the left corner, a Bradford pear tree was beginning to bloom, its small, delicate white flowers peeking out among the foliage. In a few weeks the dogwood would follow suit, dotting the landscape with pink blossoms. As he shut off the car, Greg relaxed. Despite some second thoughts about coming to Hampton Roads, he thought he might be okay after all. He was glad to be home.

A couple of miles away, not all the town's citizens felt the same about the future of Great Bridge or the role they might play in it. As Greg had driven over the bridge and past the locks of the Intracoastal Waterway, a local council meeting was beginning just a few blocks away at city hall. All six city council members were there, as was Ethan Greeley, who had been mayor for twelve years and hoped to add another term in November. But some of the council members had other plans, and the meeting, which the mayor usually controlled like a ringmaster in a cage full of circus lions, was not going well.

He stood at a podium, a wooden gavel in his right hand. The meeting room had a cozy feel to it, since members of the public rarely showed up for meetings that dealt with mundane matters such as garbage pickup. But an issue not on today's agenda threatened to change all that. Councilman Myrtle had insisted on being given a chance to speak about a resolution he was proposing. Not all the council members were inclined to agree.

Deloris, the only female member, objected. "We haven't discussed adding this to the agenda, and, besides, it's premature to pass any resolutions until the legislature has a chance to clarify this issue," she explained.

"It's all right, Deloris. The chair will recognize Councilman Myrtle," the mayor announced. As far as the mayor was concerned, postponing this battle would only make things worse. He wanted to face it up front and not be sideswiped by it.

Jonathan Myrtle rose from his seat and strode to the front to address the other members. His face was bronzed, even though summer was still months away. Not a single jet-black hair was out of place, although most men his age sported at least a little gray, and his Southern accent was perfect, perhaps a little too perfect. But that was Jonathan. He always made a sincere effort to impress the uninitiated. As for those who got to know him, they tolerated him. After all, he was a gentleman and courteous even to his enemies. He would have fit right into the pre–Civil War South—not that he was prejudiced, but he seemed to have no love for the twenty-first century as a whole. He paused before his colleagues and straightened his tie, which did not need straightening, before he spoke.

"Mr. Mayor, distinguished councilmen—uh, excuse me," he said, bowing to Deloris, "I meant to say 'councilpersons.'"

Deloris smiled at him, but it was not a happy smile.

"I'm sure you've all read the news about the DC Court of Appeals and their decision concerning the matter of Tulloch ditching," he began. "Many of us in Great Bridge have observed the extraordinary recent growth in housing starts and consider our community fortunate to be a participant in the rapid expansion of our tax base. However,"—and here he paused for effect—"many of our local businessmen have complained bitterly about unnecessary regulations and red tape. Now that the court has removed one of the biggest barriers to maintaining job growth in our little town, I'd like to propose that we tackle the backlog of residential permits that have been accumulating over the past year.

"And for those who may be opposed to continued job growth in our community because of some unfounded concerns for the Chesapeake Bay," he added, "I would like to remind those persons that I myself am dedicated to preserving our environment. When we needed additional funds to maintain the headquarters at the Dismal Swamp Refuge, my vote could be counted on. But surely we can strike a balance between jobs and our natural heritage. Certainly Great Bridge has done more than its share to reduce runoff into the bay. After all, the greatest source of pollutants are not in our small community but to the north, in Norfolk, and to the east, in Virginia Beach," he said, gesturing in those directions. His outstretched arms gave him the appearance of a tent preacher calling forth his congregation to accept the Lord. One of the council members covered his mouth and coughed to cover his amusement at the image. "In the end, we must protect our tax base, and expand it, if we are going to provide good jobs and good schools for our citizens. And come November, the voters will remember who voted for the 'special interests' in the eco-movement and who stood by their neighbors. You've all seen my written proposal. I move that we vote on this resolution urging the Department of Residential Works to speed up the approval process on these building permits." Jonathan smiled and gazed at the members before returning to his seat.

"I'd like to propose that we postpone this vote until the state legislature has a chance to respond to the court ruling on Tulloch ditching," Deloris said even before Jonathan had finished taking his seat.

"Mr. Mayor, I must object," Jonathan said, rising from his seat. "My proposal at least deserves a vote."

"Can we at least hear what Deloris has to say?" a third council member chimed in.

"I'm not sure I understand what this 'Tulloch Ditching' is all about," another member, Todd Brison, suddenly added.

Several voices either responded or argued before the steady tap of the mayor's gavel brought them to an uneasy silence.

"Ladies and gentlemen, let's conduct ourselves as a mature government body. The citizens deserve no less," the mayor urged. He glanced around and, satisfied, began. "The chair recognizes Deloris Charlotte," he said, and he pointed to Deloris with his gavel.

"Thank you, Mr. Mayor," she said, and then she turned to face Jonathan, who sat two seats down. "Jonathan, I understand that we are in the midst of a housing boom right now, and everyone is thankful for that. But I don't think we need to tear up our remaining wetlands by draining them in order to satisfy that demand. And even if we were inclined to ignore the environmental effects, there's the issue of excessive growth. Our schools are overcrowded by fifteen percent beyond their maximum capacity. We've been forced to use trailers to hold over two dozen classrooms. A sudden influx of new housing will only make that worse and might even degrade the quality of life that has drawn so many people to our community. Certainly we can give the commonwealth a chance to clarify the situation before we approve a whole lot of building permits that we might not be able to honor," she explained.

"May I?" Jonathan asked, looking at the mayor.

"Before you respond Jonathan, for those of us who are unfamiliar with the controversy over Tulloch ditching, I'll just offer an overview," the mayor intervened. He then directed his attention to the entire council. "Tulloch ditching is simply a way to drain fields and nontidal wetlands in order to make them fit for residential or commercial building. It involves digging a series of ditches so that water can drain off the land. It was named for an army colonel named Tulloch, who served in the Army Corps of Engineers, which has jurisdiction over the clearing of nontidal wetlands."

"You mean *had* jurisdiction," Jonathan interrupted. "That mistake has now been corrected, thanks to the DC Court of Appeals. I merely wish to help our local businessmen make a decent profit and create jobs for our citizens."

"But I understand that the governor is conducting a study of wetland usage in Virginia through the Chesapeake Conservancy. Once that study is done, the commonwealth will establish new rules to regulate wetlands. Perhaps we should wait for it before acting," another councilman added.

"Time is money, gentlemen and ladies," Jonathan countered. "If we waited for every study before making a decision, government would grind to a halt."

"I don't know. I think I need to learn more about this issue before I can make an intelligent vote on any resolutions. I'm sorry, Jonathan," Todd said apologetically.

"There, you see?" the mayor added. "It seems we all need to look at this a little more closely before we pass any new resolutions. Now, I understand your wife is a member of the Chesapeake Conservancy, isn't she, Jonathan?" the mayor asked.

"Yes, but I don't know what that has to do with anything," he said.

"Well, perhaps she could come to our next council meeting and explain the issue to the whole council. She might even know something about this study. After all, her father is good friends with the governor," the mayor said.

"Perhaps, perhaps not," Jonathan said, dismissing the suggestion that his wife might know anything about the study. "But if we are going to have my wife speak for the Conservancy, may I suggest that we also hear from the business side of the argument? I'm sure my good friend, Mr. William Meyers, would be happy to explain to the council some of the difficulties he goes through every time he wants to build a family home for our community."

"A reasonable request. So be it. All in favor of hearing arguments for and against the use of Tulloch ditching at the next council meeting, say Aye," the mayor commanded. A chorus of "Ayes" filled the room. The gavel came down with one sharp rap. "The ayes have it. This meeting is adjourned," the mayor finished.

He smiled to himself. He had dodged a bullet once again. But he knew that Jonathan wouldn't be satisfied until he had his proposal voted upon. He would have to face him down then, and although the mayor thought he could muster the votes to defeat the resolution, he wasn't sure he could muster the votes in November if Jonathan decided to run against him on this issue.

All these thoughts ran through his head as the council members filtered out of the meeting room, and the janitor began folding the chairs. He was cordial as he shook Jonathan's hand. Jonathan made a point of shaking everyone's hand, even those who might vote against him.

He kept his friends close and his enemies closer, if only to keep an eye on them. That made him dangerous, maybe even deadly. A man to be treated, like a snake, with respect, however distasteful that was to accomplish.

As he shook the mayor's hand, Jonathan was not concerned with the impression he had made on his political opponent. He was concerned with his wife, Ashley. But not because of the study, which he knew she was working on for the Chesapeake Conservancy. That potential thorn in his side had recently taken a backseat to more pressing matters. As he walked out of city hall to his car, he fingered a document that had been given to him just before the council meeting began. Through touch alone, he knew it was a legal document, and through experience, he knew that the man who had given it to him was a document server with the family court.

"A present from your wife," the man had said as he handed it to Jonathan, who pocketed it without a glance. But now that the meeting was over, he could ignore it no longer. He knew, even without looking at it, what it was and what it contained. Ashley had asked him to seek counseling, warned him that they had been drifting apart for years. Her words had fallen on deaf ears as Jonathan made one excuse after another.

"After the election, we'll get this all taken care of, sweet," he had said, as though a broken marriage was like a leaky faucet or radiator that you simply patched up so you could be on your way again. To Jonathan, it was—a simple problem that needed attention when time allowed.

But now Ashley had followed through on her implied threat, never saying directly what she would do but being subtle, which suited Jonathan's style. Oh, yes, she had been subtle, and he had understood, but he assumed that she would come back to him, as she had so many times before.

Except this time she wasn't backing down. It was that organization she was involved in, the Chesapeake Conservancy, that was to blame. She had gotten involved last summer, and Jonathan, busy with planning his election bid, had encouraged her, never suspecting what it would lead to . . . a wife set on her independence instead of supporting his career, and now this study of the wetlands. He wasn't even sure that he could influence her to give it a pro-business slant anymore, not at this stage.

But one thing he knew: a divorced councilman who was always stressing family values had little chance of successfully running for mayor of Great Bridge. He could handle any other obstacles in his political path, but not this one.

As he started his car, he pulled out his cell phone. He would just have to win this battle, one way or another, he thought. He would call Ashley, they would meet— for dinner, perhaps, or lunch the next day—and he would get her to pull the divorce filing. But first he needed to call Bill Meyers and tell him how the council meeting had gone.

Bill wouldn't be pleased, after counting on Jonathan's help to get his development approved. After all, he was a big contributor and had even helped Jonathan raise funds for his upcoming mayoral campaign. The land developer would have to come to the next council meeting and put a human face on this situation. The phone rang five times before connecting to Bill's voice mail, and Jonathan left him a short, terse message.

"Bill, it's Jonathan. We need to talk," he said, and he hung up.

Where could he be? Jonathan wondered.

William Meyers was far from his cell phone, which lay on the front passenger seat of his black Grand Am. The car window was open, and he heard the distant peal of the phone, but he was ankle deep in muck and mud forty yards from the road, in a very wet field that he was having drained. Let the voice mail pick it up. He had more pressing concerns at the moment.

The ditches he had dug at the site of his latest development were taking a long time to drain. At this rate, Drummond Estates wouldn't be ready for the builders until August or September, several months behind schedule. He might have to seek another delay on his loan payment to the banks. But he might be able to blame the Great Bridge city council, unless Jonathan had managed to convince them to approve the permits in today's council meeting.

Another concern crossed his mind. Ashley. She had called him this morning and asked him to meet her for lunch the next day. It was important, she had said, and even asked him not to mention it to Jonathan. Now, what could that mean?

He had been friends with Jonathan and Ashley Myrtle for many years. And it wasn't like her to keep secrets from her husband. Perhaps she needed his advice. He'd heard rumors that their marriage was going through a rough spell. Well, he'd find out soon enough.

Right now, Drummond Estates was all that mattered. If he could pull this off, he'd be set for life. Three hundred houses would be built on these lots as soon as the land was dry and the permits approved. He had sunk every penny and a lot from the bank into the project. If everything went right, he'd retire a multimillionaire. Then he could think about Ashley and other pleasures. A gentle breeze had kicked up, and the scent of honeysuckle drifted to his nose. He was following the pleasant scent and admiring the view here, at the edge of the Dismal Swamp, when he frowned. Someone was walking along one of the ditches toward him, carrying a small sack and wearing a backpack. He had forgotten that the property was not yet posted as private, and he resented this intrusion, but he decided to hold his temper. Anger was a problem for him, his wife had warned him, and although this man looked like a drifter, he might simply be a hiker out enjoying the view. He decided to give him the benefit of the doubt.

"Afternoon," Bill called out pleasantly. But the stranger was in no mood for it.

"Do you own this land?" the stranger demanded, halting just a few feet from Bill. He stood six feet tall, a good two inches taller than Bill, and wore a long brown beard. His clothes were cotton, long and light, and he wore a broad-brimmed straw hat to keep the sun out of brilliant blue eyes filled with hostility. Bill decided to play this one easy until he knew what the man wanted.

"Why do you assume I own it?" Bill said with a shrug. "I don't even think it's posted," he confessed.

"Oh," the stranger replied, and his demeanor relaxed. "I figured you were the one who dug these ditches."

Bill kicked some dirt with his foot. "Smell that? It's honeysuckle. It's a lovely day, isn't it?" he offered, changing the subject.

"Nice enough," the man agreed. Then he stuck out his hand. "I'm Earl Thompson."

Bill shook his hand and replied, "Bill Meyers. Pleased to meet you." He glanced at the sack Earl held in his left hand. "Whatcha got there, Earl?" he asked, forcing a nonchalant tone into his voice.

Earl held up the sack. "Some water samples I took." He shook the bag gently, and the sound of glass tubes jostled together reached their ears.

"Water?" Bill asked perplexed. "We got plenty of water around here."

"Yeah, but these samples I take every month. I'm studying the water quality of the swamp, to see if it changes." Earl looked at the ditch next to them. "These ditches are going to ruin the water table if the digging continues. Do you know"—he turned to Bill again—"that these wetlands filter and clean the water for the swamp and all the rivers that flow out of it, including the Northwest River? That's where Great Bridge gets its water supply," he said.

Bill folded his arms and appeared to concentrate. "Well, I thought we had chlorine and water treatment plants to take care of our city water."

"It's not the same. Someone's planning on building houses on this land. That's why the ditches are here. That'll mean fertilizers, oil spills, and chemicals, all flowing from the development and into the swamp. It'll ruin it," Earl lamented.

Bill shrugged again. "People gotta live somewhere, don't you think?" he asked. Inside, he was seething at the self-righteous arrogance of this eco-nut, as he thought of him.

Earl nearly shouted as he answered Bill's innocent query, the veins in his neck taking form like red lightning bolts. "These ditches are a crime against nature!" he exclaimed.

"Easy there, tiger," Bill said. He backed away a step and held up his hands as though fending off a physical blow, but he continued to smile.

"Sorry," Earl apologized, as the red left his face. "I get emotional about it sometimes. But things are gonna change for the better around here."

"Oh, how's that?" Bill asked.

"We're working on a study of nontidal wetlands, like this one," Earl began. At Bill's puzzled look, he added, "The Chesapeake Conservancy, that is. Well, it's almost finished, and the woman working on it is going to hand it right to the governor. If he keeps his campaign promise, it'll mean the end of Tulloch ditches like this one," Earl said proudly.

It was time to leave, Bill decided. "Well, good luck to you, Earl," he said. He turned and headed back to his car through the thick mud, seething as he struggled to remain calm. *Very interesting*, he thought. *Sometimes it pays to play dumb.* He would have to find out from Jonathan about that so-called study. He wasn't about to let some green activists put him out of business. *Say good-bye to your swamp,* Bill thought. He waved to Earl, climbed into his car after shaking off his boots, and revved the engine.

As he reached the main intersection, another disturbing thought struck his mind and caused him to brake, sending a cloud of dust from the dirt road into the air. Wasn't Ashley active in the Chesapeake Conservancy? Could she be the woman Earl spoke of? A chill went down Bill's neck as he recalled Ashley's urgent request to see him.

Earl watched the man climb into his Grand Am and thought how wasteful the six-cylinder engine on a car like that was. People never considered the consequences of their actions, he lamented. *Well, at least we can save these wetlands.* Whoever owned this land, Earl thought, was about to get a big surprise when Ashley was finished with her report. She had suggested to him just last week that it was ready. Only a few loose ends to tie up, she had said, and then smiled at him.

Earl liked Ashley's smile, liked a lot of things about her. The way her eyes glistened when she spoke to him, the way she would be working at her desk and sometimes catch him watching her from his own desk across the hall, and then wink at him before returning to her work, as though they were sharing a delightful secret. The late-night talks about the Bay and how important she found her work, how she found solace in her visits to the swamp, some of which he had taken with her.

He recalled that she rarely mentioned her husband, indeed, admitted that they had grown apart. He had begun to bring them both bagels in the morning before the day's work would begin, and they would butter them and eat them eagerly while they discussed the report she was working on.

As their daily routine became more personable, it seemed to him that they shared more than only their work, and perhaps she was just waiting for him to make the first move. It was pretty clear that her marriage was over, but he couldn't expect her to say so out loud. Yes, he would have to make the first move. He had seen the divorce filing, where she had left it there on her desk, a few days ago. She would need a shoulder to cry on.

Was she trying to send him a signal? That must be it. It didn't even bother him that she was ten years older than he was. They would make a perfect couple, he thought. He began to whistle to himself as he walked the rest of the way to his truck at the end of the dirt road. Dust coated the windshield of his truck where the Grand Am had sped by a few minutes ago, but he wasn't going to let it bother him. All was as it should be, and he was beginning to imagine his new life with Ashley. They'd make the perfect couple, he thought again. He was looking forward to seeing her in the morning, and he remembered, as he got into his truck, that he had to stop at the store for some fresh bagels.

Chapter Four

Greg watched the deer emerge from the underbrush just a few yards from where he'd paused in the early-morning silence. This unexpected surprise made his work worth all the headaches. He rested on his haunches as the deer continued to feed along the edge of the Portsmouth trail. He slowly stood but froze when the deer shot a glance at him. In a moment it returned to its feeding, and he stood up straight, easing the stress on his knees. He wished he had brought a camera. Even a disposable one would have given him a decent shot of the doe, which stood a mere twenty yards away. That, he thought, was a picture he would love to share with Amanda. She had definitely flirted with him that morning at breakfast, and he could still feel a warm glow where she had touched his arm in the middle of a hearty laugh.

Suddenly the deer jumped, and Greg frowned as the crackle of his radio in the truck spooked the animal, which scurried off the trail and back into the depths of the swamp. Greg walked back to the truck, eyeing the tracks that had caused him to stop in the first place. He was pretty sure a bobcat had made them. They were too large to belong to a house cat, and the absence of claws showing made the identification an easy one. Cats retracted their claws when they walked, even wild ones. He reached in through the open window and pulled the walkie-talkie out.

"Greg here," he said into the bulky instrument. He held down the reply button and spoke again, "Is that you, Cindy? It's Greg. Over."

"Greg, we might have a missing woman lost in the swamp," Cindy's voice replied between bursts of static. "Someone at her office said she borrowed a co-worker's truck and went into the swamp yesterday, leaving her car behind in the parking lot. They came to work this morning, and her car hadn't been moved."

"Well, what about the truck?" Greg inquired.

"That's the strange thing about it. The truck turned up yesterday evening back at the office."

"Then she must have returned it," Greg said, frustrated. He had more than his share of false alarms, and he hated the thought of bothering Floyd down in Florida unless a real emergency occurred. It wouldn't be the first time someone had called in a search team for no good reason.

"Well, her husband said she didn't come home last night, either. Should we call Floyd?" she asked.

Greg could sense the uncertainty in her voice. "No," he quickly replied. He didn't want his boss to think he couldn't handle a simple search team. "Call everybody into the office. We'll get the facts and then divide up the trails for a search. Call the sheriff's department while you're at it. I'm on my way. Over and out."

"Roger, Greg. Didn't take long for us to spice things up, did it? Over and out."

Greg smiled as he hopped into the cab and turned the truck around. Cindy sounded more confident now that a plan had been formed. He felt it too. As he headed out toward the refuge headquarters in Suffolk, Greg could feel adrenaline pumping through him for the first time in months. He was looking forward to a challenge, although this crisis might turn out to be a false alarm. Still, it was better to be safe than sorry. He had to treat this as a real emergency until he learned otherwise.

As he stopped to lock the gate at the Portsmouth Ditch entrance, he scoured the ground. It didn't look as if anyone had come through here in quite a while. The only tire tracks were obviously several days old. They could eliminate this trail for the time being.

Along the way, he turned into the entrance to Jericho Ditch and checked for vehicles. There were none in the parking lot, but fresh tire tracks suggested someone had been there recently. He stepped out long enough to examine the gate and discovered it was closed, but the

lock was undone. He doubted it had anything to do with
this missing woman. Still, he ducked between the
gate's wide metal bars and looked up and down the trail
with a pair of binoculars. Nothing caught his attention
except a generous number of monarch and swallowtail
butterflies dancing in the morning light, feeding off the
wildflowers that bloomed along the open trail. Greg
hurried back to the truck and continued south down
White Marsh Road toward headquarters.

He skipped the Washington Ditch entrance. Since it
was a favorite starting point for visitors, they would
have to search it. A small house, not much bigger than a
trailer, with a large BEWARE OF DOG sign, sat at the entrance. The dark windows and unkempt yard gave it the
look of an abandoned structure, but the presence of a
dog in the yard, tied to a large oak, betrayed that appearance. He would have to question the owner, but
time didn't allow for it right now.

At the intersection of White Marsh Road and Desert
Road he turned left and sped past small farms dotted
with aged silos that towered between the cotton fields.
The fields still sported spindly, waist-high cotton plants,
many of them dotted with fluffy white balls of unpicked
cotton.

A few minutes later, he pulled into the parking lot of
the refuge headquarters and saw three trucks and two
other cars. It looked as if most of the staff was assem-
bled. He walked in to find them in the conference
room, crowded around the nicked table, most of them
standing.

"Great Bridge deputies are on the way," Cindy said before he could even ask.

The rest of the crew looked at Greg as though lost. He missed Floyd already.

"Good," he replied. "What do we have so far? Any more information on this woman?" he asked. People shook their heads, but one field manager pointed to Cindy. Everyone looked at her.

"Just what I've told you. Her office called and said she never showed up, and that she was in the Dismal Swamp yesterday. They wanted to know if we'd seen her," she confessed. Her extended hands, palms up, suggested she had nothing more to add.

"How about her husband? You mentioned his saying that she never came home last night. When did he call?" Greg asked, coaxing information from her as quickly yet as politely as he could.

"Actually, I called him," Cindy admitted.

"You?" Greg said in surprise. "The husband didn't think it suspicious that his wife didn't come home last night?"

"I didn't ask why. He just said that the last time he saw her was the day before yesterday. He said he called her to have lunch, and she was out. Her office also told him that she was here at the refuge."

"And where does she work?" Greg asked.

Cindy glanced down at her notepad while fidgeting with the pen in her right hand. "The Chesapeake Conservancy," she replied.

"I know that group. They come here a lot. Usually

it's the field observer, Earl something—I forget his last name," Pete suddenly chipped in.

"Let's find out his name, and if he knows anything about this, and who exactly said she was coming here. Cindy?" Greg looked at her. She was moving her hand over the phone when it rang. She paused, picked it up, and before she could even announce herself, pulled the phone away from her ear. A stream of shouts laced with a few choice four-letter words blared in to the room from the handset. Greg took the receiver from Cindy.

"Get a trail map, the big one from Floyd's office," he said to Pete, who moved off accompanied by Brad. Then he turned his attention to the phone. "Who is this?" he demanded.

"This is Jonathan Myrtle, and I want to know what you're doing to find my wife!" a deep voice shouted in a thick Southern drawl. "Who the devil is this? Where's Floyd?"

"The refuge manager is unavailable. This is Greg Parnell, special agent with the National Wildlife Service. As a matter of fact, we're organizing a search for your wife at this moment. If you can give us a description of her and tell us what she was wearing, Mr. Myrtle, that would be of some help to us, sir," Greg responded calmly. There was no need for two people to lose control.

"What difference does it make what she's wearing?" the voice said in frustration and anger.

Brad and Pete had arrived with the map and spread it on the table.

"Sir, if we know, for instance, that she doesn't have a coat, we can inform our searchers in the field to be prepared for treatment of hypothermia or other conditions requiring first aid. Now, I know you're upset, but believe me, if your wife is in the swamp, we'll find her, and any information you can give us could be useful," Greg said.

There was a pause on the line. "I suppose you're right. I'm a little frantic, that's all."

"I understand, sir. But if we all keep our heads about us, we'll find her much sooner. I'm going to give you to our radio operator, so she can take a description, which she can relay to our team in the field. Hang on, sir," Greg urged, and he covered the mouthpiece before the caller could reply. "Take it in Floyd's office," he said to Cindy, who nodded and headed out of the room. As soon as Greg heard her pick up the receiver and begin speaking, he hung up his extension.

"Enough of that," he muttered, and he glanced at the map. He did a quick head count—five workers—which left Cindy to cover the phones. "Everyone have his radio?" Greg asked. Some raised their hands, some mumbled or nodded, while one or two actually fumbled for the walkie-talkies on their hips, as if to confirm by touch their equipment's presence. "Good," Greg affirmed. Then he looked over the trail map, leaned in close, and began to throw out assignments.

"Pete, you take Randy and head for the Washington Ditch. Split up, and one of you head up the Lynn Ditch until you hit the Jericho Ditch. The other one heads for the lake. Brad, you and—I'm sorry, what's your name again?" he stumbled. A couple of days had not given him enough time to memorize all the names.

"Sarah," the ranger replied.

"Sorry, Sarah. You and Brad split up at the Jericho Ditch, one take Jericho, the other take Hudnell Ditch to Camp Ditch, and meet up at the intersection of Camp and East Ditch, right here," he explained, pointing to the map. "I'll take Williamson Ditch and meet you there. John, you follow me up Williamson and then head up East Ditch, and check out North Ditch, then head back to Jericho." Greg looked around the room. "Is that everybody? Cindy. Where's Cindy?" he asked. Then he saw her in the doorway, clutching a notepad. "Good, now how many deputies are we getting?" he asked.

"Uh, two to start, but I guess we can ask for more," she said.

"That's fine. As soon as they arrive, send them down Railroad Ditch and then West Ditch, and have them follow that to Interior and then to the lake. That should cover the major trails for now. We'll check out South Ditch later if necessary. Combinations. Everyone have the combinations to their gate? Cindy, make sure those deputies know the combinations to the gate locks. Good," he finished. He looked around the room and asked, "Any questions? Ideas? Suggestions?"

"Oh, one more thing. Some guy out bird-watching said he saw someone, driving a white pickup, try to break out of the swamp through the Washington Ditch gate," Brad said, and he pulled a note from his pocket.

"A woman?" Greg asked hopefully.

"No, a man. And it happened yesterday," Brad added.

"Cindy, check back with the husband and see if his wife was with someone or traveled alone to the swamp," Greg said.

"Odd, though, that someone would try to break out of the refuge. Wonder how he got in?" Brad speculated.

"Maybe he forgot the combination, or came in by another gate. Anything else?" Greg asked. He surveyed the room.

All heads shook in the negative. "Okay, let's find this woman—what's her name?" he asked, glancing at Cindy.

"Ashley Myrtle," Cindy replied, referring to her notes.

"Right, okay, keep in touch by radio if you find anything and when you've reached your destination. Let's go get her," Greg asserted.

"What about Portsmouth Ditch?" someone asked as they headed out.

"I was there this morning and didn't see any sign of her, but if we come up empty, we'll take another look." There was a brief logjam at the door as everyone tried to leave the room at once. Then they exited for their vehicles. Greg was the last to clear out. He turned and said to Cindy, "Keep in touch."

"I'll let you know when the sheriff gets here," she assured him, and then she smiled and gave him a quick thumbs-up.

He smiled back and headed out the door.

Chapter Five

The trail system in the Great Dismal Swamp Refuge is built upon two-hundred years of logging, draining, road building, and farming. Many of the earliest roads were built by slave labor under dangerous conditions, when malaria, poisonous snakes, and cholera were more likely to send a man to his grave than old age. But between the slaves and the greed, the changes to the swamp took effect, and millions of feet of lumber were removed, mostly of cypress and cedar. Cypress and Atlantic white cedar are rot resistant, making them valuable for roof shingles and particularly for shipbuilding.

Even the waters of the swamp, stained the color of tea due to the presence of decaying vegetation and acid from the juniper and cypress roots, were said to have medicinal qualities. The acid in the water hindered the growth of bacteria, making it ideal for long voyages aboard whaling and trade ships. Many a crew slaked their thirst from the waters of Lake Drummond, whether in the port of New Bedford or four thousand miles away under an endless, rolling horizon of ocean in the South Pacific. It could even be argued that the economic success of the American whaling industry owed much of its longevity to the Great Dismal Swamp.

But the swamp could only give so much, and today it was only a third of its former size. Once, it stretched from the Outer Banks in the south to the Chesapeake Bay, and in the east from Virginia Beach, fifty miles west to the Suffolk Escarpment. Even today, it enclosed over one hundred square miles of tick-infested wilderness, and only the presence of the trails kept hikers from becoming lost in the seemingly endless sea of trees, briars, vines, and muddy waters. Step off the trail, and the swamp looks the same in all directions. Lose the sun on a cloudy day, or forget your compass, and you can plan on spending the next several hours in the Dismal Swamp. If you're lucky, you'll find your way back to the trails with a few cuts and bruises. If not, you'll spend the night in the swamp, maybe two, if the searchers don't catch up to you. And if you haven't found religion before you get lost in the Dismal Swamp, you will before you leave . . . that's guaranteed.

By all accounts, Ashley Myrtle was familiar with the swamp, which left Greg with an uneasy feeling in the back of his mind. Surely, if she'd been here before, she would have a map, or at least know enough to stick to the trails. Perhaps she had gotten complacent, wandered away from the trail in pursuit of something that caught her eye, and then turned around to discover, too late, that she was lost. It seemed hard to believe, but Floyd had assured him that even experienced hunters occasionally lost their way in the bogs and depths of the swamp. The best outcome Greg could picture at the moment was a quick rescue, with a dirty and disheveled woman muttering apologies to the search party. Better yet would be if the whole thing was a false alarm. As Greg approached the end of Williamson Ditch, those thoughts reassured him. He waved to John, whose truck headed north while he turned south along East Ditch toward the rendezvous point. As he drove, he checked the small canal that ran parallel along most of the trails for broken foliage or any other signs of human disturbance. Once, he stopped and stepped from his vehicle to examine the ground. Several nicks and cuts in the soft soil— as if a struggle had occurred?—caught his eye. He surveyed the ground and quickly saw that the area was dotted with hoofprints, from one or more small deer. A little farther away, he found the prints of a predator, most likely a bobcat. Greg imagined the scenario: two deer fed, while a large bobcat stalked then charged its prey. A bit unusual but not unheard of, since the bobcat was at the top of the food ladder, except for human hunters. A large bobcat would be more than a match for a small deer. The absence of drag marks suggested that—this time, at least—the deer had escaped.

Maybe next time, Greg mused. He'd like to see a bobcat in the wild, but not today. Prints or scat were the only sign most people ever caught of this elusive hunter. Greg climbed back into his truck and continued down the road. As he came around a bend, a large blue heron, disturbed by his presence, took flight. The creature gave its piercing, prehistoric cry before disappearing over the tree line. His window open, Greg began to notice that the air was full of the songs of warblers, woodpeckers, and hawks. Turkey vultures, circling high overhead, were the only silent winged presence. A plane buzzed over the south a mile or more away, which gave him a new idea. Perhaps they could hire a small plane to cover the ground more quickly. Certainly, if Ashley Myrtle were in the swamp, she would follow the sound at least to a trail, which would make this search end with smiles all around. Greg reached for the radio and paused to listen to some chatter from the other searchers.

"Cindy, it's Brad. Are you there? I found her," Brad radioed. Slamming on his brakes, Greg pumped a fist, and a broad smile broke across his face. It would be quite a story to tell Floyd.

"I'm here, Brad," Cindy responded. "Do you need an ambulance?"

"Roger that. Where are those deputies?" he asked.

"They're on their way to Railroad Ditch."

"Send them over here, and the ambulance," Brad said. His voice was strangely somber.

"Brad, it's Greg. How's she doing? Over." Then he added, before Brad could respond, "Cindy, where's the nearest hospital, Suffolk or Great Bridge?"

"Greg, not the hospital," Brad replied.

"Great Bridge is closer." Cindy's voice crackled on the radio.

"We're not going to the hospital," Brad replied.

"Why not? Is she all right? Over," Greg asked.

"She's . . . she's dead. She's dead, Greg. Over," Brad finally confessed.

Greg let the radio slip from his grasp. The strength fled from his fingers, and his head dropped against the steering wheel. What was he going to tell the husband? What was he going to tell Floyd?

"Greg, are you there? Over. Greg?"

For a moment, the sounds of the truck and the radio and the birds and animals in the woods around him were drowned out by an overwhelming feeling of despair. *I failed,* Greg thought. *I failed, and I'll get the blame, just like last time.* The incident in the Army came rushing back to him—the rash decisions, the mistakes, the reprimand. *Low man on the totem pole takes the fall,* he thought.

"She's dead. Greg, do you copy? Over."

Chapter Six

It took him several moments to regain his composure. He had to stay focused, he told himself. His confidence returned when he reminded himself that in the end, despite the mistakes in the Army, he'd been right. He had been right then, and he wouldn't assume the worst now. He steadied his hands on the steering wheel, then picked up the radio and barked into it.

"Brad, don't touch anything. Start CPR if you can. Cindy, alert the sheriff we'll likely have a body, do you read me? Over."

The replies were quick in coming. Greg put the truck into gear. He felt he was back in charge. He drove along Camp Ditch until he saw another truck about half a mile ahead of him. Sarah's vehicle, he surmised. It went around the bend and was lost to his sight at the spot where Camp Ditch intersected with Jericho Ditch.

About one hundred yards farther up Jericho Ditch sat Brad's SUV, and beside it, a plastic tarp draped over a body on the trail. Greg saw, without even asking, the drag marks where Brad must have jumped into the chilly water to retrieve her.

Brad sat in his vehicle, wrapped in a blanket, his soaked shirt and pants on the ground. Sarah handed him a cup of hot coffee from a Thermos she carried. The others arrived as Greg surveyed the scene. Everyone wore a glum face. Randy stood, hands on his hips, waiting for instructions, while John scanned the edge of the canal.

"No chance of CPR?" Greg asked through the driver's side window. Brad just shook his head.

"She's been in the water for over twelve hours, judging from the looks of her," Sarah said. "I was a paramedic once," she explained at Greg's quizzical expression.

That was it, then. Greg knew that even in rare cases where hypothermia had lowered a victim's temperature enough to slow the body's metabolic rate, the chances of saving a life diminished to zero after a couple of hours in cold water, and they were never that good even before that. Although miracles happened, he didn't see it happening this time. The rest of the search party was arriving, and Greg knew that the ambulance and sheriff's deputies would have to operate on the narrow trail.

"Randy, can you stay with me?" he asked. Randy nodded. "Brad, you should get back, get warm and dressed. Sarah, can you go with him?" Greg asked. "Everyone else, I think we're done here. We'll just need the ambulance and deputies. Let's make some room for them to do their thing," Greg announced.

As if on cue, the deputies' vehicle appeared a couple hundred yards north, headed toward them. The deputies pulled into a turnaround one hundred yards above them to let the other cars drive past, and then continued to where Greg stood. The ambulance was now visible, and it gently maneuvered past the caravan headed north back to the refuge exit.

Greg shook the deputies' hands and introduced himself. The older deputy, Tom Bentley, had a shock of white hair that stood up when he removed his hat. He must have been nearing retirement age, and he looked as if this was a part of the job he wouldn't miss in the least. The other, Ron Green, sported a thin black mustache and was easily a dozen years younger than his partner. Judging from his age, early- to mid-forties, he might have been one of the first black deputies hired by Great Bridge, whose sheriff's department hadn't accepted minority applicants until the mid seventies. Even in the smallest Southern towns, the color line had finally broken down.

They waited until the ambulance pulled up and two paramedics stepped out and brought a gurney from the vehicle. Greg pulled the tarp off and got his first look at the woman they had all hoped to find alive. The paramedics moved in and checked her pulse. One of them recoiled at the first touch of the cold arm before placing two fingers on her icy white wrist. The other paramedic unbuttoned her shirt, placed a stethoscope on her chest, and listened briefly before making it official.

"She's dead," he simply said.

Until now, Greg had been watching the proceedings with regret disguised as cynicism. But suddenly he stooped down beside the man and studied the woman's lifeless arm.

"Get some plastic bags and tie them around her hands," Greg almost shouted. "Don't remove anything—dirt, anything—until the coroner examines her," he ordered. He looked closely at the hand and used a pencil to gently reveal a small petal beneath the button of her coat sleeve. He was about to mention it when he suddenly realized that everyone was watching him, dumbfounded, as though he had gone crazy. His face reddened, and the hairs on his neck tingled. After several tense moments one of the deputies broke the silence, to Greg's relief.

"All right, you heard the man. Let's bag it up. Treat this area like a crime scene," Ron ordered. The paramedics gathered some plastic bags, and Tom, the other deputy, went to the trunk of his car.

"I've got a camera," Greg said, and Ron nodded. He followed Greg back to his truck just as Greg emerged with his Pentax ZX-30 and flash. He placed a hand on Greg's shoulder and asked in a low voice, "It's just a drowning, isn't it?"

"Probably. But . . ." He hesitated. He didn't want to reveal his suspicions just yet.

"Okay, it's your find. You're in charge," Ron conceded.

"We should search the area then, go through the drill."
Greg nodded affirmatively.

"Hang on there, gentlemen. We're gonna search the
perimeter. Could you wait by the ambulance for just a
few? Thank you," Ron said. Tom returned with some
evidence bags and a handful of small flags. He placed
the first one next to the body.

"Okay, let's check for footprints before we mess anything up," Greg said. He, Randy, and the two deputies
started in a line and surveyed the area while the paramedics stood by their ambulance, looking bored. At
the edge of the water, where Ashley's body had been
pulled, Greg pointed at a boot print. Tom pushed a flag
into the ground next to it. Greg took two pictures of the
print, getting close up for the second shot.

"Could have been Brad, the guy who found her, but
better be safe. I've got some plaster of Paris in my
truck. Randy, can you make a cast?" he asked. "Sure,"
Randy replied, and Greg handed his keys to him.
Randy motioned to Pete, who went to assist him.

Greg took pictures of the canal where she was found,
the Jericho Trail from both directions looking north and
south, and a tire tread that was too close to the edge to
have been made by any of the vehicles present. He then
turned his attention to the body. He stood above the torso
and stepped on the edge of the blue camping tarp that
was used to cover the corpse. He angrily kicked at the
edge of the tarp, then bent down to pick it up and tossed
it clear of his work area. He knelt down by the body and
studied the delicate features. Even now, after twelve

hours of exposure to the elements, in a swamp filled with hungry creatures that prey on the dead, he could still see the graceful beauty in her swollen face. He could almost imagine that she was asleep, resting in some peaceful dream. He pulled brown, curly strands of hair off her oval face and smoothed them out, then leaned next to her ear and whispered, "I'm sorry."

"Did you say something?" Ron asked as he turned and looked down at Greg.

"No, just muttering to myself. I'm ready to record her. I might need some help," Greg said. Ron nodded, and Greg took the first picture. As Greg gestured, the deputy held up the arms and hands, as Greg snapped away. Then he snapped the head, face, torso, and lower body. He stared at the feet, covered with comfortable walking shoes, and took a picture of them.

"Did you see her nose?" Greg inquired. "Did you think it looked a little funny?"

"Like it was broken?" Ron suggested.

Greg nodded and snapped a frontal close-up. He hesitated and then lay down on the trail next to her and snapped a profile of her face. "Could you hold her lips apart?" he asked. Ron gently pulled her lips open with rubber-gloved hands, and Greg snapped a photo of dirt-encrusted teeth. "Are any broken?" he queried, referring to Ashley's picture-perfect dental work.

Ron glanced back and forth as though examining a prize horse at a farm auction. "Not that I can see," he conceded after a moment's hesitation.

Greg grunted. As he rose, he brushed off his legs and

water-soaked knees. "Well, I guess that's it. Anything else you think we should cover?" Greg asked the deputy.

Ron shrugged, not willing to state an opinion that he might later be forced to defend, and merely added, "It's your show."

"Can I get a pair of those?" Greg asked and pointed to the deputy's latex gloves. He pulled on the gloves that Ron offered him and carefully removed a small petal from beneath the button strap on Ashley's right sleeve.

"Can you bag this?" he asked Tom, who held several plastic evidence bags in his hands. Tom opened a smaller bag, and Greg dropped the petal into it. He accepted the Magic Marker from the deputy and wrote on the bag: *Ashley Myrtle flower petal right coat sleeve Jericho Ditch 1/4 mile north of Camp Ditch, GDS March 15.*

"Thanks," he said, and he handed the marker back. "I'd like to keep this," he added. "Our lab in Oregon can identify it."

"Um, we'll need you to sign for that, to preserve the chain of custody," Tom said hesitantly. Then he thought better of it and turned to his partner. "We can't turn this over to USFW, can we?" he asked.

Ron shook his head. "Better ask the coroner about that. I can't make that decision. Not to say your lab isn't qualified and all, but . . ." he explained to Greg.

"No problem. I'll ask him about it. I want to go in with the ambulance anyway," Greg conceded.

"Thanks," Ron said. "Frankly, if it was up to me,

heck, I'd say yes—we could use a little help—but we're just a couple of deputies."

"That's okay. I don't want to step on any toes," Greg said. Then he added, "Hey, Deputy," and waited for Ron to turn and face him. "Don't sell yourself short. I was once a lowly PFC, and look where it got me," he joked with a smile.

Ron smiled and saluted before he returned to his car.

Greg looked at the ambulance driver. "She's all yours, gentlemen." He stood and watched while the paramedics placed her in a zippered body bag and loaded her onto the gurney. As the metal table slid into the back of the ambulance, he hopped into his truck and prepared to follow it to the morgue.

Chapter Seven

The morgue was in the basement of the Great Bridge municipal building, which also housed the mayor's office, city council offices, and administrative offices. If you wanted to appeal your property assessment, file a will, or even get a fishing license, you could walk right in without an appointment. The basement was reserved for those whose walking days were over. Even the sign announcing its location was small, old, and minus a few coats of varnish. Greg had to ask someone where to find it, and even she had to ask someone else.

Finally, he walked around the corner from a small office marked ANIMAL CONTROL and tugged at the basement door, which creaked noisily as it swung open. His hand touched the right wall as he stepped slowly down the poorly lit stairwell. As he reached the bottom step, a short, stocky man emerged from around a corner, his face buried in a manila folder. His eyes rose from the papers just in time to see Greg, and he skidded to a stop on the well-worn ceramic tile.

"Whoa," he muttered and smiled. "Didn't hurt 'cha, did I?" he said, and his eyes danced behind half-rimmed spectacles that threatened to slip off his nose and on to the floor, though they first would have bounced off a rather large belly.

"No, I'm fine. But I'm not really familiar with this place," Greg explained.

"Not a problem. First time in the morgue, eh? Welcome to the bowels of our domain," the man uttered with enthusiasm. "Need some help, or is this just a social visit? We love getting visitors around here."

"Actually, I'm looking for the coroner," Greg said. He thought the man was somewhat odd.

"Ah, I should have figured from the uniform," the man said. He ran his eyes up and down Greg's lean, tall frame. "Follow me, and I'll take you right to the big man downstairs." His shoes clattered on the floor with his quick steps, while Greg's boots and slower pace made a more muted contribution to the echoes in the hallway.

"Been working here long?" Greg asked. The man who hurried before him wore a white shirt with thick vertical gray stripes, charcoal-gray pants, and a silk tie of royal blue. The professional look was marred by wrinkles in the pants, a tie loosely pulled away from the throat, and shirtsleeves rolled up to the elbow, revealing very hairy arms.

"Oh, I've been here for a few. Leastways, long enough to learn the layout of the place," he admitted.

"Know much about the coroner? What's he like?" Greg asked.

"Him?" the man said with heightened interest. "Oh, he's a pip, that one. You'll like him," he said with a gravelly voice that actually sounded as if it held a smile.

They turned another corner to the left and passed a room with double doors. One door was open. Inside, Greg sighted a body bag on a stainless steel table. *The cutting room*, he thought.

They arrived at the end of the hallway and entered a large office through a door with gold leaf lettering marked CORONER.

"Here it is," the man stated, and he dropped the manila folder onto the desk. The room was brightly lit and dominated by a large mahogany desk, on which sat an in-box holding a short stack of paper and an out-basket that was empty. The radio softly played a violin concerto by Bach. To Greg's left was a corkboard on the wall with numerous Post-it notes and assorted other papers held to the cork with a selection of colored pins. The far-left bottom corner of the corkboard held a collection of pins that formed the outline of a hangman's scaffold. The wall on the right side of the room boasted several wooden bookcases containing a wide range of subject matter. Most of the books related to criminal law, forensic science, and medicine, although some of the shelves bore various works of nonfiction and biographies, particularly of musical figures from the Renaissance to the modern jazz period. There were even a few examples of fiction and poetry. A copy of Dante's *Inferno* caught Greg's eye. He uttered a short whistle.

"What a great collection," he said, still perusing the shelves. "This guy must be pretty interesting."

"Thank you. I try to keep on my toes," the man said from the leather swivel chair behind the desk. Suddenly, Greg realized the man he had been talking with was none other than the coroner himself. He greeted Greg's look of astonishment with a quick chuckle, followed by an outstretched hand, which Greg shook eagerly.

"Ken Schmidt, Great Bridge coroner, at your service. What can I do to you?" he asked.

"Greg Parnell, Fish and Wildlife Service," Greg replied. He hesitated for a moment, then queried, "What did you ask me?"

"Never mind," Mr. Schmidt responded, and he waved a hand. "Just a little joke I like to play. To what do I owe the pleasure?"

"I'm investigating the death of a woman who was found in the Great Dismal Swamp Wildlife Refuge. She should have been brought in this morning. We have a probable name, Ashley Myrtle, subject to ID, of course," Greg began.

"Oval face, brown curls, light-blue Windbreaker, khaki pants, Reebok walking shoes?" Ken asked.

Greg nodded, and Ken slapped a hand down on the desk on top of the manila folder he had been carrying. "It's all there—well, what I got from the ambulance crew, anyway. Care for a look-see?" he asked. Ken pointed to a chair, which Greg fell into while he glanced through the report. It didn't contain anything new, although he noticed the plastic evidence bag with the flower petal was attached to the inner cover, held with a paper clip.

"Have you determined a cause of death yet?"

"My initial draft says death by drowning, unless any new information comes to light," Ken replied. His fingers waltzed through his beard.

"I thought as much, although I suppose the autopsy will confirm that. When will that be? I'd like to watch, if you don't mind," Greg said.

"Hold on there, young feller," Ken said, and he made a quick snap of the wrist as if holding an invisible whip. "Crack," he cracked. "There ain't gonna be an autopsy, 'less the next of kin requests it, or unless the coroner—yours truly—feels the need for one. And so far, I ain't feelin' the need, if ya get my drift. And most people, 'specially 'round these parts, feel the same way about cutting up loved ones that they once felt about Northerners."

"I just assumed there'd be an autopsy. I mean"— Greg tried to explain his thinking—"isn't that standard procedure when a death occurs with no attending physician?"

"Well, in your larger cities, among modern police departments and such, that's probably the rule of thumb," Ken began. "But around here, where everybody knows everybody else, we do things a little less formally, and with good reason. We don't have a lot of anonymous killings, strangers whacking strangers, so to speak. We know most of our locals, and when they die, we usually know what done 'em in," Ken said. He raised his eyebrows several times in a small dance. "Not to say your philosophy's the wrong one. But it probably doesn't apply here."

"I see," Greg said, hiding the disappointment in his voice.

Ken Schmidt picked up the tone, however. "Not that we don't get to do autopsies from time to time. I'd be glad to call you when we get a John Doe case, or someone requests an autopsy. Oh, then you'll see a real pro at work. Why, I've got a bread knife that could slice a single millimeter layer off a full-size liver with one stroke. Want to see it?" Ken asked. Before Greg could respond, Ken hoisted his briefcase onto his desk, undid the clasps, and removed a leather sheath. From this he pulled out a long blade by an ivory handle, with a glistening edge that sparkled under his desk lamp. He examined it in the light, and Greg sat up to get a closer look.

"Be careful! It's razor sharp," he warned as Greg reached for the handle.

"She's a beauty. Had it a while?" Greg asked. He was impressed with the edge, especially since the style of the knife suggested it was quite a number of years old. The handle had a carving depicting a pair of pronghorn and a bison in full stride.

"I've had this beauty for almost twenty years. A present from my missus," Ken said proudly. "Won't let any-one use it but me. I sharpen it myself with a whetting stone."

"It's not really a—?"

"A bread knife? Naw, that's just a nickname we med-ical folk use," Ken explained.

"Well, it's not that I want to see any old autopsy, but the cause of death in this case concerns me. I suspect it might be more than just a simple case of accidental drowning," Greg confessed as he handed back the knife.

Schmidt returned the blade to its sheath and snapped shut the briefcase before responding.

"Think she might have had a little help, do ya? Any particular reason?" Ken asked. "Wouldn't have to do with that flower I received with the body, would it?"

"Actually, yes. That and the fact that the truck she was driving when she went to the swamp made its way back to her office without her."

"Hmm, that's a nifty trick. Sure about that, are you?" Ken quizzed him.

"Well, that's what I've been told by her co-workers," Greg confessed.

"Uh-huh," Ken stated with little satisfaction. "Straight from the horse's mouth is the best source, I always say, but she won't be telling us anything now," Ken said, and he nodded toward the folder on his desk.

"That's why I'd like to get that flower petal examined. Any chance I can send it to our USFW lab in Oregon? They specialize in identifying plants and animals."

"I don't think we can do that," Ken said, his tone suddenly cautious. His fingers again stroked his beard, but now slowly and methodically.

Greg took a chance. "Oh, come now, Mr. Schmidt," he said with a smile. "A man who appreciates Bach's Violin Concerto in D would want to know if he has all the pieces of the puzzle before reaching a conclusion, even if he's just curious."

"You're familiar with Bach, are you?" Ken asked, and his face lit up.

"My dad was a big fan of classical music. When we were growing up, there was usually something from the Baroque period on the record player. He had most of the masters. I prefer jazz, myself. But when it comes to classical, I lean more toward Aaron Copeland and John Adams, personally," Greg replied.

"The Americans? I like them too, but for really great music you can't beat them Krauts!" Ken said with delight. He eyed Greg for a moment and then said "Tell you what I'll do. You give me the address of your lab in Oregon, and I'll ship it there on ice, from this office. We'll pick up the bill to boot. How does that sound?" Ken asked.

"Thanks a lot. It may be nothing, but I'd like to be sure," Greg said. He wrote on a page from his notebook and then ripped it out and handed it to Ken. "I also have a roll of film from the scene. I'll get double prints and give you a set," Greg added.

"Fine, fine," Ken said, and he shook Greg's hand as they both stood.

"One other thing. Could you let me see your final report?"

"Sure, sure. It won't make the best seller list, but I think it'll keep your attention."

"Great. My number's on there as well," Greg said.

He found his way back up to the first floor and decided to wait before calling Floyd. So far he had no definite proof that this was anything other than an accident, but he wasn't satisfied. The coroner seemed to feel it was a closed case, and Greg couldn't see the man wanting to hide anything. *Perhaps I'm being paranoid,* Greg thought. Why would anyone want to kill a harmless woman in a backwater swamp?

Chapter Eight

Thanks," Greg said as he took the pictures from the clerk.

"Are you a cop?" she asked.

"Yeah, with Fish and Wildlife," Greg replied.

"Oh, I guess that explains it. I was wondering why someone wanted double prints of a body. I never saw one before," she confessed, and she shivered.

"Not my favorite part of the job," Greg admitted. He decided to wait until he was back at the refuge headquarters before reviewing them, although the temptation was strong. As he drove, it occurred to him that, other than at funerals, he'd never seen a dead body either. Even when his father had died suddenly, Greg had been in college and hadn't seen him until the wake. Perhaps that was why he'd felt so angry when first viewing Ashley Murtle's corpse. Now that a little time had passed, he felt calmer and was running down a list of things to do—visit the victim's husband, her office, and debrief the staff who had been at the scene. He would also have to call Floyd sooner or later. Greg wasn't sure if USFW even had jurisdiction in this case. It might belong to the Great Bridge police, perhaps even the FBI. A phone call might clear that up. *Add that to the growing list*, he thought.

He pulled into headquarters and rushed into the building, noting an unfamiliar car in the parking lot. No one, to his knowledge, drove a late-model blue-gray Lexus sedan. Not even Floyd Culpepper, the refuge manager, could afford a vehicle like that. He greeted Cindy, who pulled him aside.

"There's a man from the FBI waiting for you in Floyd's office," she whispered.

Scratch one chore off his list, Greg thought. "Good. That'll save me a phone call. Anyone else around?" Greg asked.

"Sarah and Brad—the rest of the team is back in the field," Cindy explained.

"Okay, send them in, would you? I want to review these photos, and they might as well see them too."

"And I called Floyd," Cindy added. At Greg's look, she grimaced and said, "Sorry. I didn't mean to steal your thunder."

Greg shook his head. "I just didn't want him to think I was ignoring him."

"Actually, I had to leave a message. He was at the hospital with his mom, so you'll still get to fill him in," she said with encouragement.

"Thanks," he said with a smile, which earned one in return.

He entered Floyd's office to find a tall, broad-shouldered man studying a map of the refuge. The man wore a dark-blue suit, red tie, and white shirt. His hair was in a crew cut. That, along with a thick neck, served to give his head a bulletlike appearance, the shape interrupted only by a strong chin. He turned when Greg entered the room and extended his hand.

"Greg Parnell? I'm Dan Brennan, FBI," the man explained.

"Pleased to meet you," Greg said, and he shook the offered hand firmly. "Didn't expect to see you so soon," he added with mild surprise.

Greg sat at Floyd's desk while Dan sat opposite him. "I suppose you want to see these?" Dan said, and he held out his credentials. He slipped them back into his suit coat pocket at the wave of Greg's hand. "We got a call from the Great Bridge sheriff's department when your missing woman turned up dead. Since she was found in a Federal refuge, we got involved," Dan explained.

"That's just as well. I was about to look over these photos from the crime scene," Greg said, dropping the pictures onto the desk.

"Crime scene? The way I understand it, this was an accidental drowning. Sounds pretty routine," Dan said. Greg noticed that he made a quick glance at the watch on his wrist as he spoke.

"Well, I'm not sure about that," Greg said with some hesitation. "What office do you work out of anyway?"

"We're in the Norfolk office," Dan said, crossing his legs. Greg noted the Bill Blass dress shoes. "This is more or less a courtesy call, you know. To see if you need any help."

"Slow day at the office, huh? How'd you get the short straw?"

Dan frowned. He suddenly became more attentive, leaned forward, and asked, "Aren't you a little young to be a . . . what did you say your title was?"

"I get that a lot," Greg explained, and he sat back in his chair, straightening his shoulders. "I'm a Special Agent with the US Fish and Wildlife Department."

"So, you're kind of like a game commissioner, right? Or a forest ranger?" Dan asked. His voice held a hint of condescension.

"Actually, I'm a field agent," Greg countered.

"A field agent? Out where the buffalo roam? What kind is that?" Dan asked.

Greg leaned forward and folded his arms on the desk. "The kind that tracks poachers in ten-degree weather through two feet of snow, armed with a. 30–06, because the guy you're up against is also armed to the hilt, and there's no cell towers or backup around to help you if you get into trouble. No FBI agents either, but that can be a blessing, not a handicap," Greg added with sharp eyes.

Dan played stonefaced, and then his nonchalant expression widened to a slight smile. "Fair enough, Special Agent Parnell. I'm just here to offer my assistance . . . if you want it," he added with a subtle tilt of the head.

Greg smiled. He relaxed and leaned back in his chair. "Actually, I was planning on calling you, and yes, I'd appreciate any help you can offer."

As this apparent truce was reached, a knock on the open door frame caught both men's attention. Sarah and Brad stood at the door.

"C'mon in, guys. Meet Special Agent Dan Brennan," Greg said as he waved them in. They shook hands all around while Greg removed the photos from their sleeve. He passed a set to Dan and shared the second with Brad and Sarah.

"Anything you can add to what we saw this morning, speak up," Greg urged. He passed the photos one at a time to Brad, who then gave them to Sarah.

"Who found the body?" Dan asked.

"That was me," Brad explained. "I was driving down Jericho Ditch when I noticed a break in the foliage that lines the banks of the canal. It didn't look right, so I stopped. When I got out, I saw her blue Windbreaker. At first I thought it was garbage, until I noticed her hair. I just dove in and pulled her out. I started CPR but realized after a minute that she'd been dead for several hours."

Greg snapped his fingers. "Where's that cast—you know, of the footprint I found by the water's edge?" he asked. Brad rose and left the room for a moment while Greg fingered through the rest of the photos and pulled out his snapshot of the boot print to show to Sarah and Dan.

"How do we know it wasn't made by someone at the rescue scene?" Dan asked.

Brad returned with a large cloth and set it heavily on the desk. He unwrapped it to reveal a cast of a boot print, which everyone bent forward to examine.

"I've already eliminated our staff," Greg explained. "I still need to talk with the sheriff's deputies who were there, but I'm sure they didn't leave it. They seemed to know crime scene procedures pretty well."

"She was wearing some kind of sneakers," Dan mused as he held up a photo, "so that eliminates her." He returned his attention to the cast. "What do you make of the style? I've seen that logo before."

"Timberland. I have a pair myself," Greg answered.

"It has a distinctive wear pattern on the sole. We shouldn't have any trouble identifying this if we actually find the match. May I take this and ship it to our lab?" Dan asked.

Greg thought for a moment. "To tell you the truth, I don't know. It may fall under local jurisdiction."

"Are they investigating?" Dan asked.

"They seem to think it was just an accidental drowning," Greg admitted. "Open and shut."

"A drowning?" Dan asked skeptically. He pulled a picture from the middle of the pile and passed it to Greg. "Looks like some bruising on her face. Did you take this close-up for any particular reason?"

"The sheriff and I thought her nose looked broken," Greg said.

"And her teeth were dirty, as if she'd been shoved in the mud," Brad added. "I actually had to pull a lump of dirt out of her mouth, trying to give her mouth-to-mouth."

"Where is it?" Dan asked excitedly. "Did you save it?"

Brad's face turned red. "Should I have? I thought, I mean, I didn't think that was important," he confessed.

Dan frowned but then tried to hide his disappointment. "Well, it might have given us something, maybe DNA, but there's no guarantee. It couldn't be helped."

"There might be more, still, in her throat maybe," Sarah said. She reached over to squeeze Brad's arm, lending a measure of encouragement.

"Good point. When's the autopsy?" Dan asked, turning to Greg.

Greg shook his head. "I already talked to the coroner. He's satisfied that it was an accidental drowning."

"Hmm," Dan muttered. "These locals don't waste any time, do they? Can you give me his number? I might need to talk to him. Personally, I think you've got more than enough evidence here for an investigation. "Nice work," he added, and he surveyed the room, making quick eye contact with everyone. Greg smiled, and Brad and Sarah mumbled their appreciation for the compliment. Dan pushed the photos together and stood them on end, tapping them into a neat pile. "Oh, one more thing. What's the significance of this?" he asked. He held up the photo of Ashley Myrtle's sleeve.

Greg pointed to the flower petal he had photographed. "I believe this flower is a woodland species, which doesn't grow around water. In fact, it doesn't grow anywhere near where her body was found . . . if I've identified it correctly."

Sarah glanced at the photo over Brad's shoulder.

"That looks like a petal from the dwarf trillium!" she exclaimed. "Good grief, I've never seen one before, except in pictures. They're quite rare, you know."

"That's what I thought," Greg admitted, "but I wanted to be sure before I said so."

"What's the significance?" Dan asked, and then he tapped his forehead. "Of course," he said in answer to his own query. "She might have been killed elsewhere and her body moved. Can you prove this flower is whatever you said it is?"

"The coroner agreed to send the petal to our forensics lab in Oregon. They specialize in identifying flora and fauna. If anyone can identify it, they can. I was going to scan this photo and e-mail a JPEG to a friend of mine as well, see if he couldn't give me a positive ID."

Dan nodded slowly. "Not bad, Special Agent," he said with a smile. "You would have made a fair FBI man," he teased.

"So, I take it we've piqued your interest."

Dan stood and handed him the photos. "Enough to recommend to my supervisor that we open a file on this one. Can I get copies of all the evidence you've collected?"

"You can probably have ours," Greg said. "I've got to call my boss, but I don't think this is in our jurisdiction. He'll probably be eager to drop this into your lap."

"Still, I might need your help, seeing as she was found in the refuge," Dan admitted.

"Anything you need, just ask," Greg said.

"Good. Thanks again," Dan said to Brad and Sarah.

Greg escorted him to the door. "I'll let my boss know that you're investigating. He'll be relieved, I think. He doesn't need a lot more on his plate right now."

"You feel the same? I was planning to visit the dead woman's husband, get his statement. Interested? After all, you guys did find her," Dan conceded. "Unless you've got something better to do, like count turtles or something," he cracked.

Greg's expression must have given him away.

"Right. I'll wait in the Lexus," Dan said. Greg nearly trotted back into the building and yelled, "Cindy, I'll be back in a couple of hours." He entered the parking lot just as Dan pulled alongside, and Greg heard the click of an electric door lock being opened.

Chapter Nine

Jonathan Myrtle lived in a rebuilt section of nearby downtown Portsmouth, near the banks of the Elizabeth River, in a section known as Old Towne. A few years ago, unwilling to follow so many other urban downtown areas into decay, the city fathers had undertaken a massive investment to turn the city's history and architecture into a showcase of stylish apartments, eateries, shops, and art galleries. Although a few blighted areas remained, the centerpiece of this effort, High Street, had become an important draw for families, students, artists, and tourists.

As Dan and Greg emerged from the downtown tunnel that carried them beneath the muddy waters of the Elizabeth River, Portsmouth revealed herself. From High Street, Dan turned left onto Dinwiddie Street, past a four-story hotel of the same name that had seen better days. At the end of the street, Dan pulled over next to a three-story apartment building with white pillars that framed the royal blue doors that marked each separate apartment unit. A dogwood stood guard in front.

"Here's the address," Dan said. They got out, and Greg noticed a dark-haired man with a sun-bronzed face sitting in a rocker on the porch, one hand around a glass of iced tea. His hair was cut short, and he wore a dark-gray suit, despite the warm day. He took no notice of them until they had climbed the stairs and stood in front of him.

Dan was the first to speak. "Mr. Myrtle? I'm Dan Brennan, special agent with the FBI, and this is Greg Parnell, with the Fish and Wildlife Service."

He looked up at Dan with moist, weary eyes. He didn't answer but merely gestured toward two chairs across from his rocker. He set his iced tea on a small table nearby. A set of wind chimes tinkled as a breeze toyed with it. They waited a moment. Greg wanted to express his condolences before Dan started asking questions about their investigation, but Mr. Myrtle still took no note of them, and Greg felt the opportunity either hadn't arrived or had already been missed, like the fleeting glimpse of an animal in the evening dusk.

Then Jonathan Myrtle finally spoke. "Fish and Wildlife?" he asked, looking at Greg.

Greg nodded.

"You must have been one of the men who found my wife," he said.

"Yes, sir, and I want to say how sorry I am for your loss," Greg said.

"I do appreciate that," Myrtle announced. "Both of you, thank you for coming." He addressed Dan as well, then returned his gaze to the street, where children were playing hopscotch, and a pair of men changed the tire on a Chevy Corsica.

"Many's the morning when Ashley and I would sit here on the porch and drink iced tea before the day got started. I bought this building twenty-five years ago. It was fallin' apart back then. Took us a few years of hard work to get it into shape. Just sold the whole thing for a half million dollars last week. Wish she could have been here today," he said sadly. "It's such a nice day."

"Is there anything we can do for you?" Greg said suddenly. He thought this probably wasn't the time for an interview. Perhaps another day would be better. He was about to suggest that to Dan, when, to his surprise, Dan jumped in with both feet.

"Mr. Myrtle, I realize this isn't the best time for this, but we have a few questions we need to ask you," Dan said, drawing a notebook and pen from his suit coat.

Myrtle glanced at him quizzically. "Did you say you were with the FBI?" he asked.

"That's right, sir. And I was just wondering—"

"Why would the FBI be visiting me about my wife?" he asked, almost to himself, and placed a hand to his chin. He turned and looked at Greg. "You, I can understand, but—" He turned to face Dan, the sentence left unfinished.

"Well," Dan said, clearing his throat, "your wife died

on Federal property, and Fish and Wildlife is not really equipped to investigate this.

His explanation only seemed to baffle Jonathan Myrtle more. "What?" he asked.

Dan straightened himself in his wicker chair, which continually threatened to slide him unwillingly onto the porch. "That is to say, we're investigating your wife's death, and we just need to ask you a few questions, if you don't mind," Dan explained.

"Perhaps," Greg said, standing, "we should come back tomorrow."

Dan's face displayed his feelings about that, but Jonathan took the ball from them both.

"It's all right, gentlemen," he said. "Although I don't think I can help you. The coroner's the man you want to see." He glanced at Greg and added, "I do appreciate your condolences, however." Then he tapped his forehead. "Where are my manners? Can I get you gentlemen some tea?"

"That's okay, I don't need anything," Dan replied.

"I'm fine," Greg said.

Jonathan Myrtle nodded and then spoke. "I had four hundred dollars to my name when I left home. But I worked hard, saved my money, and bought my first building—this one. And of course, met my wife, whom I married twenty-four years ago. This week would have made twenty-five," he said wistfully. He sighed and then added, "Along the way, I've learned a thing or two about people. What have you learned, Mr. Brennan?" He returned his gaze to Dan, who studied his host intently.

"I've learned," Dan began, while he kept his gaze on Jonathan Myrtle, "that your wife's death by drowning may not have been an accident."

Jonathan's expression changed from certainty to confusion. "How's that?" he said, and for a moment his veneer cracked. He turned to look at Greg and asked, "Is that what you think as well?"

Greg shifted forward in his seat. "It's just that, well, we can't assume anything until we've examined every possibility, Mr. Myrtle. Whenever there's a death without an attending physician, we need to investigate. I'm sure you understand."

Jonathan shook his head with vigor and pulled himself back in his chair, raising his height a couple of inches. "No, no, gentlemen, I'm afraid you misunderstand. There's no mistake, although I wish I could blame someone for my wife's death. But the truth is, her own stubbornness did her in."

"Hers, or someone else's?" Dan quickly countered.

"What exactly do you mean, sir?" Jonathan asked, his voice stern, almost threatening.

"Well, for instance, the initial report that Special Agent Parnell received stated that your wife drove to the Dismal Swamp Refuge in a borrowed white truck, which later turned up at her office. I'm not a physicist, but I know that vehicle didn't drive itself back to her office."

"Is that true?" Jonathan inquired, turning to face Greg.

Greg affirmed it with a nod, then added, "We still need to question her co-workers about it, but—"

"Well, then, you still have some people to interview.

I won't hold you gentlemen up any longer," Jonathan concluded, seizing the opening to end the interrogation.

Dan directed a look of dismay at Greg, paused for a moment, and then began to rise from his chair. Greg placed his cap, which he had been cradling in his hands, on the table, and he shook Jonathan Myrtle's hand as the two men rose.

"I'll keep you apprised if we learn anything," he said, to which Jonathan muttered his thanks.

Myrtle then shook Dan's hand and held it for for several seconds while he spoke. "My wife was always venturing into that swamp, often alone. I didn't like it because I was afraid something like this might happen one day. When you two are done, I'm sure you'll come to the same conclusion the sheriff did."

"Why are you so sure, if you'll excuse the question, that your wife accidentally drowned?" Greg asked.

Jonathan placed a guiding arm on the younger man's shoulders as he escorted the lawmen to the steps of the porch. "Because my wife," he explained, "didn't know how to swim." He nodded as he caught Greg's surprised expression, while Dan wrote in a notebook.

"Wait, wait a minute," Dan begged as he finished scribbling. "Your wife couldn't swim at all?" he asked with genuine surprise.

"Not a stroke," Jonathan replied. "With all her projects and charity functions, it's just one of those things she never got around to learning."

Chapter Ten

"That's great. What a great interview," Dan complained, once they were back in the Lexus. "And you didn't help things any, handing him that opening to end it," he added.

Greg lowered his head. "Yeah, that was kinda dumb," he admitted.

"All right," Dan said. "So, we got off track with the interview. Looks like it doesn't matter anymore. She obviously slipped and fell into the canal. She couldn't swim and must have drowned," he said as the car pulled away from the curb. From his seat, Greg got his last glimpse of Jonathan Myrtle, seated once more, watching the street.

"I'm not so sure about that," Greg mused aloud. "I came here today thinking we'd meet a grieving widower, but he handled us pretty well. We may have to interview him again."

"I'm gonna check out his explanation—you can count on that," Dan said pointedly, steering with one hand and gesturing with the other as they sailed through the downtown tunnel leading back into Norfolk. "But if his wife really couldn't swim, that pretty much seals it. My boss won't see much point in opening a file on her death without something more to go on."

"I guess you're right, but I still would like to get a confirmation from my lab in Oregon. I'm sending them an e-mail with some scanned pictures attached, see if I can get a preliminary ID on the evidence we pulled off her coat."

"What, that flower petal? Is that really so significant?" Dan asked. His voice signaled a sense of defeat.

"I thought you said we did a good job, had a lot of stuff to go on," Greg said with impatience and mild despair.

"That was before I found out she couldn't swim!" Dan exclaimed. He lowered his voice and added with a sigh of futility, "Man, we got nothing, or next to it. I'm not even sure I see a crime here anymore." He glanced at Greg, who looked as glum as he felt. He tried to encourage him and said, "I'll go over everything I saw with my supervisor and see what he says. Maybe he'll see something to go on."

"If he asks you what you think, what are you gonna tell him?" Greg asked.

"I don't know yet," Dan said slowly after a few seconds' hesitation.

Both men were silent as the car headed south on Interstate 464.

Then Greg spoke up. "Is that your final answer?" he asked with a grin. Dan laughed. The subject switched to sports, as both men buried their own doubts about the case in a heated discussion on the Norfolk Tides and their chances for the upcoming season. It was still in full bloom when Dan drove into the refuge headquarters to drop off Greg.

Cindy looked up from the desk when she heard a car in the parking lot, and a moment later Greg walked through the front door of the Dismal Swamp Refuge headquarters.

"You're still here?" he asked.

"I didn't know if you had a key," she said.

Greg tapped his forehead. "Duh! Sorry to keep you waiting. I should have called, but actually, I'm glad you're here. Do we have the Oregon lab's e-mail address?" he asked.

"The forensics lab? Sure, but why?" Cindy asked.

"A guy there owes me a favor, and I want to send him some pictures. Do we have a scanner, I hope?" he asked from the conference room. He emerged with the pictures and pulled the three he wanted.

"In Floyd's office," she said, directing him. She followed and pulled a cover off a flatbed scanner that sat on a table behind Floyd's desk. "It hasn't been used in a while, but I think I remember how to work it."

"Oh, I could stumble through it, if you need to get out of here," Greg said.

"What, and miss the most excitement we've had in years?" she joked, eliciting a smile from Greg. "Let me have those," she said, taking the photos from his hand.

"We need a pretty high resolution, in case he enlarges them," Greg added. Do we have a DSL or cable hookup?" he asked hopefully.

"On this budget?" Cindy asked incredulously.

"Oh, yeah," Greg responded. "Sorry, I should have realized."

"You young whippersnappers and your tech toys," she complained with mock dismay. "Hang on while I get this set up. I'll scan them at two hundred dots-per-inch. Anything bigger, and it'll take an hour to transmit them. Of course, Oregon's three hours behind us, so they'll still get them today," she quipped.

"Thanks, Cindy. I'll let you work. I have to make a couple of phone calls." Greg ducked back into the conference room and pulled a card from his wallet. He dialed a number, and a voice picked up on the third ring.

"Grabowski."

"Get to work, you bum," Greg said sternly.

"Hey there, Greg my boy!" came the enthusiastic response over the phone. "How are you doing, you little scallywag? Been staying out of trouble?"

"Oh, I don't look for trouble. It looks for me," Greg said. "But I'm not complaining, Pete."

"I heard a rumor you took a transfer to Region Five. Where'd they put you? New York, Philly, maybe? I understand the chicks are pretty hot out there on the East

Coast. Gettin' yourself a little wildlife on the urban side, eh?" Pete ribbed.

"Actually, I took a tour in the Great Dismal Swamp, in Virginia," Greg said.

"The Dismal Swamp? You gotta be kidding me! What the heck are you doing there? I don't think even they get any visitors. Taking early retirement, are we?" Grabowski teased.

"Unfortunately, no. We found a body in one of the canals, a woman who went missing yesterday," Greg countered.

"Really? So what'd she do, fall off her yacht after drinking too much?" he asked.

"Not exactly. It looks like a simple drowning, but I'm not convinced. I need some help. And you remember what you said about that favor you owed me?" Greg asked, easing his way into the subject.

"Uh-oh, here it comes! I knew this had to be more than a social call," Pete said with dismay.

"You said anytime I needed something?" Greg reminded him.

"I knew I'd regret that. What is it? Need a loan 'til payday?"

"I just need an ID on some vegetation."

"No can do, buddy."

"It's three pictures."

"I got a staff meeting tomorrow, and I have to give a report."

"Just your best guess."

"I won't get 'em 'til day after tomorrow even if you overnight 'em."

"I'm attaching them as files to an e-mail."

"Has the refuge manager approved this?"

"He's out of town."

"How convenient. You know how much trouble I could get into?"

"They're claiming the body tomorrow. If I'm wrong, no harm done."

"And if you're right?"

"Well, then, I'll give you all the credit."

There was silence on the phone for several seconds. Finally Pete grunted, "This is your last favor for the year, my man."

"Right . . . until next time."

Greg heard a series of keyboard taps.

"Nothing. Well, did you send 'em already?" Pete asked.

"Uh, they're almost ready," Greg confessed.

"Almost," Pete muttered. "Get 'em over here. I leave in two hours," he added.

"They're on the way," Greg said. He wrote down Pete's e-mail and gave him the headquarters' phone number before he hung up. He dashed into Floyd's office just as the last picture was scanning.

"I kept the ruler in the scanned photo, figuring you'd need it," Cindy said. "Here's the folder where I copied them, under that woman's name, Ashley Myrtle."

"Excellent," Greg said. "Do you do windows also?"

Cindy laughed. "Unfortunately, yes. Well, there you

are," she said, and she moved out of the chair to allow Greg to sit down. In ten minutes, he had sent the e-mail with three attachments and had called Pete to confirm they had been received. As he hung up the phone he gave a sigh of either relief or apprehension—he wasn't sure which.

"And now?" she asked.

"Now, we wait," he said, and he looked at his watch. It was 6:30 P.M.

"Well, have fun," Cindy said. She handed him a key. "Lock up when you go. I'll see you tomorrow."

"Thanks, Cindy. Thanks for everything," Greg said as he walked her out.

"Good luck," she said. She smiled and left.

Greg returned to Floyd's office and sat down. He would probably be having a late dinner, but he didn't think of leaving and missing Pete's call. A short walk to the vending machine yielded a bag of Fritos, some cupcakes, and a cola. He pulled out a few reports on the status of the Great Dismal Swamp that Floyd had written last year and which he had suggested Greg review. He read while he ate and slowed his chewing whenever he found a passage of interest. He soon ran out of interesting material and food as well. Boredom set in, and he actually found himself yawning once or twice. Although it was not very late, darkness had already fallen. He almost pounced on the phone when it finally rang, and as he picked up the receiver, he noted the time: 7:30 P.M.

"Greg Parnell, Dismal Swamp Wildlife Refuge," he announced.

"I lost my dog," a craggy voice groaned. "I lost my dog in the Dismal Swamp! Can you help me find it, kind sir?"

Greg was toying with a pencil and pulled a notepad within reach. Something wasn't right about this. "Um, your name?" Greg asked.

A chuckle came back in response. Greg breathed a sigh of relief.

"Had ya going there for a minute, didn't I?" Pete asked. "Are you gullible, or what?"

"No, just getting tired," Greg confessed. "Any luck?"

"Oh, heck, yeah. I got lots of luck, except it's all bad. The wife wants me to take dancing lessons, and my team lost five games in a row."

"I mean, any luck with the ID?" Greg asked.

"Oh, that? Well, just answer me this. Who's the best forensic man in the entire US Fish and Wildlife Service?"

"You are, of course."

Pete chuckled again, a soft, melodic sound that emerged whenever his ego was pumped. "Then you'll be glad to hear this. That flower petal you sent me is none other than a rare species found in low-lying eastern woodlands, called the dwarf trillium—from the trillium family, only much smaller than your typical trillium. Hardly seen anymore."

Greg squeezed a fist and smiled. "That's what I wanted to hear. What about growing conditions? What does it like?"

"Well, it's your typical moisture-loving, shade-dwelling forest flower. When we had large old-growth forests in the East, it was pretty common, but with all the trees cut down and so many deer around, it's hard to find a patch of them. The Dismal Swamp is one of the last places you can find it, until you cross the Mississippi headed west.

"So you wouldn't find it growing by a pond or a stream, for example?"

"No, no, no," Pete exclaimed. "It likes moisture, but it doesn't love standing water, and it doesn't love open sun. It's a shade plant. It needs drainage and cover. Blooms in mid-March for only a few days."

"Thanks, Pete. That helps a lot."

"Well, you owe me one now. But I'll settle for hearing the outcome of this case. Are you going to send me the actual plant, so I can make this 'educated guess' official?"

"The Great Bridge coroner is sending it to you tomorrow through his office. My name will be attached," Greg explained.

"That's all I need to know. And I'm out of here. Good luck," Pete said.

"Thanks again," Greg replied. He hung up. He looked around and lifted some papers until he found a brochure describing the flora and fauna of the Dismal Swamp. He then pulled a bent card from his front pocket and dialed another number.

"Dan Brennan, FBI," a voice responded after only one ring.

"Dan, it's Greg Parnell. You said I could call if I had anything. I hope it's not too late?" Greg asked.

"No, not really. I was just having some dinner. Hang on a second," he said. A moment later, his voice returned. "I just wanted to step away from the table. What's up?"

"Sorry to interrupt, but I got a definite ID on a flower that was found on the victim's sleeve. I'm pretty sure she was killed somewhere other than where her body was found, and I think I can prove it."

"Okay, I'm listening," Dan said.

"Well, according to this brochure the refuge publishes, the flower is only found in the northwestern corner of the swamp. That's miles from where she was found."

"Okay. But I don't see how you can prove anything by it—in court, that is."

"By going out there," Greg explained. "First thing in the morning, I'm going to search for the flower. If I find it, I might find where she died. There could be all kinds of evidence there, don't you think?"

"Hmm, I get your drift. By the way, I talked to my boss, and he didn't see any reason to open a folder on this, unless you came up with something new. I suppose, if you found the spot where she died, that would qualify. What time were you going to do this?" Dan inquired.

"As soon as it got light, around seven o'clock. Care to join me?"

A grunt told Greg that this was less than desirable, but Dan replied, "Okay, I guess I can make it."

"Let's make it eight," Greg relented. "And bring some water."

"That's better. Eight o'clock then, at the refuge headquarters?"

"Yes. I'll have a map and compass."

"Fine. I'll bring the donuts. See you there," Dan replied.

Greg hung up and stretched his arms over his head. It was getting late, and he switched off the lights and headed for the door. It would be an early start tomorrow. As he was locking up, he thought of Dan's last statement. "Donuts," he had said. Greg chuckled. "He must have been a cop once," he muttered to himself.

Chapter Eleven

Dan pulled up in the refuge parking lot at 8:10 A.M. by Greg's watch. Greg grabbed his knapsack and tossed it into the back of the nearest USFW truck. He turned to face Dan, who was walking toward him after locking his vehicle, and smirked.

"What?" Dan asked, perplexed. "I'm only a few minutes late. What's the rush?"

"It's not that," Greg said. "Where do you think we're going?"

"For a walk in the woods," Dan said. "Hey, I was an Eagle Scout. I know how to find my way around."

"Oh, well, that makes all the difference," Greg said. "No boots? Water?"

Dan pulled a water bottle out of his sports jacket pocket.

"Evian? Good choice!" Greg cracked.

"The shoes are broken in, by the way. They're more comfortable than they look," Dan said defensively. "Let's roll, Mountain Man."

They climbed into the truck, and Greg headed north on Desert Road, then turned right onto White Marsh Road. Along the way they passed hay fields and old barns, small ranch houses with fenced yards that held grazing horses, and one tractor plowing a future soybean patch. Blue sky held only a few patchy clouds, but farther west the horizon was gray.

"I just came along this road," Dan said.

"We're headed for the entrance to the Jericho Ditch, north end of the refuge," Greg explained. "It's a bit drier there. Not so swampy. That's the best place to look for what we want."

"So my shoes won't be a problem after all," Dan said.

Greg looked at him and merely smiled. "If you say so, chief."

They passed an occasional car coming south from the opposite direction on the narrow two-lane road. As they approached the Great Bridge city limits, more houses and fewer farms began to dominate the landscape. Greg turned the truck right onto a dirt road just before they reached the White Marsh Plaza. A small brown sign identified their destination as GREAT DISMAL SWAMP REFUGE JERICHO DITCH. They followed the road for one and a half miles, passing a lone house on the right, and farther along, a small trailer set back off the road with a large enclosed pen holding hunting dogs. The dogs bayed loudly as the truck passed.

"What are those dogs doing out here?" Dan wondered.

"Hunting dogs," Greg explained.

"Hunting dogs?" Dan said incredulously.

"Yeah. Hunting dogs. For hunting deer and bear. We have a short season in October to balance the deer in the refuge."

Dan shook his head. "I thought using hunting dogs went out with Reconstruction," he remarked.

"Since I'm a fellow carpetbagger, I won't repeat that statement," Greg kidded him.

"Gee, thanks, boss," Dan remarked. "Have a donut on me." He handed Greg a waxed paper bag emblazoned with a Krispy Kreme logo. Greg murmured his approval and stuck one hand into the bag.

At the end of the road, he pulled into a dirt-packed circle cut into the woods, which served as a parking lot. A large oak occupied the center, protected by four thin logs set in a square around the tree base. Greg pulled alongside the fence and cut the engine.

"Can't you open the gate and drive in?" Dan asked.

"There aren't many places to pull over in case there are other personnel in the field," Greg explained. "Besides, it's not far from here. Half a mile north along the ditch there's a bridge that crosses the canal into the swamp."

He swung a backpack onto his shoulders, tightened the pack's belt around his waist for support, and grabbed a pair of binoculars and a small camera bag from the cab.

"Here. Make yourself useful," he said, handing the

camera bag to Dan. He hopped over the thick steel arm of the gate that separated the parking lot from the entrance to the refuge, while Dan stooped down and easily passed through the wide gap between the top and center steel bars.

"Welcome to the Great Dismal Swamp, Mr. Brennan. You're standing where few modern men have stood before," Greg announced.

"Remind me to send my mother a postcard," Dan joked. "Which way, Daniel Boone?"

Greg pointed north, and the two men began walking up the Jericho trail. The morning was still cool, the sun low in the sky. Despite that, they soon began to sweat. Once or twice Greg paused to point out something along the trail, a basking turtle on a half-sunken log, a set of deer tracks in the moist soil. To Dan's eye, everything appeared as a solid wall of green vegetation, except for the brown trail beneath their feet and the black, sluggish waters of the canal on their right.

After fifteen minutes, Greg held up a hand, and both men stopped. He gazed through the binoculars and after a few moments waved Dan forward and handed him the eyepiece without a word.

Dan fixed his view along Greg's pointing arm. In the distance, two hundred and fifty yards north along the edge of the trail, a pair of deer fed on the tender grasses that grew in the open areas. Neither man spoke, but Dan grinned broadly, and Greg continued to watch them. Dan opened his water bottle and managed to polish it off in a few deep pulls.

After several minutes, Greg stepped forward and whispered, "We'd better get moving again."

They continued along the trail toward the deer, which saw them at a hundred yards and leaped back into the swamp. Clusters of butterflies danced in the air up and down the trail, feeding on flowers and sometimes less fragrant targets. Greg pointed out a small cluster of swallowtail and monarch that fought for position over a small black mass just off the trail in the grass.

"What is that?" Dan inquired.

"Scat," Greg explained. "Probably muskrat or raccoon, judging by the size. They feed off the minerals and proteins left behind undigested."

"Not exactly something I needed to know, but I'll think twice now about buying that butterfly poster for my daughter."

A small wooden bridge, tinged with moss and missing a couple of floorboards, appeared on their right, crossing the canal into the swamp, and Greg stopped and tested the first few feet with one boot. Convinced the structure was secure, he crossed, holding the railing with one hand. The bridge bounced with each step he took, and he dropped onto a cushion of pine needles and leaves with a sigh of relief.

"Is this thing safe? I'm a few pounds heavier than you," Dan announced as he gripped the railing and took a tentative step. He stopped while Greg contemplated the question.

"Well, we'll find out in a minute, I guess," Greg said

seriously, and then, in a lighter tone, added, "Just kidding. This backpack weighs thirty pounds. C'mon."

In a few moments, Dan was across, although the bridge had a little more spring in it than it did at Greg's crossing.

"Well, now we're really into the swamp," Greg announced, and he pulled out a compass, glanced at it, looked up, and seemed satisfied enough to pocket the instrument.

"Let's spread out, about thirty feet apart, and head that way," he said, and he pointed east. "Here's what we're looking for." He handed Dan a refuge brochure with a picture on it. "The plant's about two to five inches tall, leaves come in threes, as do the petals, which are white or violet," he said, as Dan struggled to see the small photo under the shade of the tall trees.

"Any questions?" Greg asked.

"You want fries with that?"

"Maybe when we're done. Let's go."

The men parted and began to walk slowly into the woods, leaving the sunlight and the trail behind them. As their eyes surveyed the ground, a vulture silently circled overhead for a pass, then drifted on the winds farther south, seeking less active prey. They paused only once, for a water break, supplied by Greg this time. They didn't speak much, and when they did, it was in hushed tones, as though they were trespassers, uninvited visitors to the swamp. Although the ground was drier in this part of the swamp, the foliage dominated by invading red maple and pine instead of the native cypress and cedar, Dan found himself dodging large pools of standing water, sometimes successfully.

Almost an hour into their search, Dan called out. "Hey, over here," he announced. Greg hurried to the spot where Dan stood pointing to the ground in front of him.

"Look, there, and more over here," he said, and Greg followed Dan's directions with his eyes. They advanced slowly, stepping over the fragile flowers to avoid crushing them, and Greg snapped his fingers. A large patch of dwarf trillium stood at the edge of a small clearing, but something had recently disturbed them. The leaves and other ground cover were pushed about, revealing the earth beneath. Some of the flowers lay crushed, and the tangled briers, which had frequently blocked their steps, appeared to have been moved aside. Greg raised an arm to halt their slow advance and then silently pointed to the ground. A faint outline of a sneaker rested just before their feet.

"Buddy, I think you may have found it," Greg said excitedly, and he carefully dropped his pack.

Chapter Twelve

"Whatever happened took place here," Greg said, and he opened the camera bag that Dan handed to him. "Watch where you step." He pointed to a tangle of weeds. "Keep away from that spot."

"What? What are you looking at?" Dan asked with a frown. He jumped back and swore. "These shoes cost over a hundred bucks!" he said to no one in particular.

"Then don't get them wet. Stay off that!"

"What?"

"You're standing on the spot where she may have been killed!"

"How do you know that?" Dan asked with exasperation. "I just see weeds."

Greg motioned him away from a tangle of wild Queen Anne's lace and pawpaw, which had been crushed close

107

to the ground. "See? Look here, and there. Someone was lying down here."

"How do you know a deer or some other animal didn't sleep here last night?" Dan asked.

"Because the ground's too wet here, and the bedding would have been too thin. That looks like a handprint!" he said, and he knelt carefully. He took several pictures while Dan looked at the area. He was beginning to understand, because he pointed to what looked like a boot print. "Hers?" he asked.

"Too big, I think. Must be a size eleven at least." He took another picture. They looked at each other.

"Are you thinking what I'm thinking?" Dan asked.

They stood and surveyed the ground. Greg explained his theory, and Dan listened, nodding once. "There were two people here. The victim must have lain down here. See the faint outline in the weeds, and the handprint at the top left corner? It's small, like a woman's."

"Yeah. And that boot print at the bottom right corner, as though he stood above her."

"Or stood up after . . . what? Killing her? That depression in the top center. She could have been facedown, and he could have sat or knelt above her, holding her down in the mud. Maybe she did drown—in two freakin' inches of water!"

"Can we get an imprint of the boot and the hand?" Dan asked, and he glanced at the sky. "I don't think they'll be here after this rain."

"I've got some plaster of Paris in the truck. But it's twenty minutes there and twenty more back."

"Give me the camera," Dan insisted. "I've got the idea. I know how to work a crime scene. I'll keep searching. You can make it ten minutes each way if you run. Got a pen? I need to make notes."

"Okay. Be right back." He handed Dan the camera and bag.

Thirty minutes later, two molds were taken and carefully lifted. The hand and footprint were filled carefully and allowed to harden. A chill went up Greg's arms as he looked at the molds and carefully placed a wet towel over them. "How did you scoop out the water?"

Dan shrugged. "I'll have you know these shoes are good for more than walking!"

Greg smiled grimly. The FBI agent who had stepped so gingerly into the brush a couple of hours before was now muddy from the knot of his Yves St. Laurent tie to the bottom of his Gucci shoes.

"Just take it out of your clothing allowance," Greg suggested, and he laughed at the hand gesture his comment elicited. "Got that one?" he asked of the other mold.

"Yeah, and while you were gone, I found and photographed this as well." Dan pulled a handkerchief from his suit pocket to reveal a muddy gold bracelet, herringbone design, with two blue pearls at the clasp. "Right by the handprint. Took a picture before I picked it up."

"Pretty unique. The husband should be able to ID it," Greg added. "Let's put these into the box."

A rumble of thunder sounded in the sky, and a few minutes later the sky opened up. Dan threw his coat over the flaps of the box. They were soaked by the time they reached the truck, but even a casual observer would have been perplexed by the broad smiles they wore as they placed the box into the cab and piled in after it.

As they pulled out of the parking lot and down the road to Route 58 and White Marsh Road, Greg slapped a hand to his forehead. "The coroner! He's supposed to turn over the body today. Can we stop it?"

Dan already had his cell phone out. He wiped the front with a wet hand and punched in the number. "I'll call him. If he won't delay, I'll tell him I can call a Federal judge and get an order for an autopsy," he stated.

"You can do that?" Greg asked as he stepped on the gas.

Dan smiled at him. He didn't reply. Then his attention was diverted. "Yes, may I speak to the coroner please?" After a moment he continued, "Dan Brennan, FBI. Yes, I'm working the Ashley Myrtle case."

Greg could hear a female voice on the other end of the conversation.

"Well, it looks like that death certificate will have to wait. I'm aware of that. May I just talk to him, please? It's very important." He covered the mouthpiece and leaned over to Greg, whispering, "She's worse than the coroner. At least—Yes, this is Dan Brennan. As I was saying to your secretary, that death certificate may need to be modified. It seems we've found some new evidence. It's a woman's bracelet, and it may belong to the victim. No, I need to show you. We're on our way. We should be there in about ten minutes."

Greg opened and closed his fist twice.

"Well, we may need to postpone turning over the body after what we have to show you. Yes, I'm sure the councilman won't like it, but I can get a Federal judge to order an autopsy."

For a few moments the only sound in the car was the sound of windshield wipers hugging the glass, but Greg could see the back of Dan's neck bristle and swell like that of a bull before a charge.

"Fine . . . I'll take full responsibility." With that, he snapped the phone closed and thrust it into his damp coat. He shook his head in response to Greg's nonverbal inquiry. They drove in silence for a minute until the buildings and church towers signified they were entering the peaceful community of Great Bridge.

Finally Dan blurted out, "These people are so stubborn! Now I know why they cling to the idea that the South will rise again!"

"Yeah, with our luck, right on top of us," Greg added.

Chapter Thirteen

They were making their way down the stairs when Dan held out a hand and turned to Greg. "Look, I know you get enthusiastic about your opinions, especially when you know you're right, but maybe I should handle this one."

Greg frowned and began to open his mouth as if to ask, *What is that supposed to mean?* But he hesitated, and a moment later a faint smile formed at the edges of his mouth. Before it broke across the lips, he nodded and said, "You wanna take this, no problem." He folded his hands in front of him, while Dan assessed the response with a perplexed look. "You okay with this? I'm not trying to criticize, but—"

"Please," Greg countered, and he extended his arm toward the coroner's office and moved back a half step. "Be my guest."

The coroner scowled when they were ushered into

his office. Dan extended a hand in greeting. Instead of taking it, Ken Schmidt pointed at him with a pen in hand and thrust it out to make his point. "You have no authority to order an autopsy in this town!"

"Please, Mr. Schmidt," Dan began, trying to maintain a calm manner and defuse the tension in the room.

"This is a local matter—" Ken continued.

"Sir, if I may—"

"And I have already ruled this death an accidental drowning—"

"And we have some new evidence—"

"And we don't need outsiders to tell us how to do our job—"

"If you could just look at this—"

"Good day to you, sir!" With that the coroner strode out of the room, ignored Dan's outstretched hand, and gave a cursory nod to Greg, who stepped back and muttered "Mr. Schmidt."

Dan stood there, hand poised in midair for another second before letting it sink to his side.

He got a pat on the back from Greg. "Nice job there, Mr. FBI," he said in a low voice. "Let's go."

The men walked back up the wide steps to the building's entrance. The light was failing, and dusk tossed shadows into corners and along long hallways. Their feet etched a lonely echo in the mostly empty building.

"Well, I may have to get that judge to order an autopsy. Better call the funeral home and make sure they don't make plans to pick her up and start pumping her full of embalming fluid yet. But first I've got to get the okay from my supervisor," he said, and he pulled his cell phone from his suit pocket.

"There's another way, maybe," Greg offered.

"What's that? Steal the body?"

Greg paused near the doors leading out of the building. To their right in a small dark foyer, an illuminated portrait of General Stonewall Jackson peered down at them like an angry god ready to repel the invaders. Greg explained his plan to Dan.

"We need to identify the bracelet, right? So, we show it to Mr. Myrtle, he IDs it, and when we tell him where we found it and that we found two sets of prints, he may see fit to letting us get that autopsy."

"Maybe. And then again, maybe not," Dan complained, still stung by the rejection they'd just received.

"Well, while we're there, we might take the opportunity to ask a few questions, see if he knows any reason his enemies might want to hurt him, get to him through his wife, you see. That might make him think."

"Enemies? How do you know he has any enemies?"

"Well, he's a successful politician," Greg explained. "He wouldn't be successful unless he had enemies. Maybe we can use that angle to get the autopsy. Do you smell something burning?"

Dan noticed it too, but before he could reply, a voice boomed from the dark corner alongside them, "That won't be necessary, gentlemen!"

They turned together toward the sound and saw a tall man rise from a chair in the waiting area just below the portrait of General Jackson. As the stranger stepped forward, Greg could see a long cigar burning in his hand. He then saw that it was Ethan Greeley, the mayor of Great Bridge. He approached them and blew a perfect circle of smoke, which floated gracefully above his dark head of hair. He extended a sun-bronzed hand to shake theirs each in turn, and then left it extended but turned it palm side up. "May I see the bracelet?"

Greg glanced at Dan expectantly. Dan hesitated for a moment, then reached into his coat pocket and brought forth his hanky, containing the gold bracelet. He handed it to Ethan, who opened it gingerly with a large brown hand. The cigar rested between the fingers of his other hand.

"Do you know what creates the color in a blue pearl?" he asked while he cradled the evidence.

"No, sir, I don't," Greg answered for both of them, although he suspected that the question was rhetorical, directed at neither of them. He wanted to be deferential, because he sensed that whatever happened next, it was wise to remain in the good graces of the mayor. He and Dan had few enough friends as things stood.

"It comes," Mayor Greeley began, "from a rare abalone called the Paua, found only off the coast of New Zealand. Now, according to the Maori native islanders, the Paua abalone had no shell, and their sea god took pity on the creature, so he gave it a shell to protect it. He made the shell from the blue of the ocean and the colors of the dawn and sunset sky. As a result, pearls taken from the Paua abalone are always blue instead of white. That's where these pearls come from," he said, pointing to the clasp of the bracelet.

"Interesting," Greg said, eager to stroke the man's ego.

"You seem to know a lot about this bracelet," Dan added. This drew a quick look from the mayor, a look that Greg couldn't place as being hostile or friendly. But the mayor's attention returned to the gold object in his hand. "I should. I gave this bracelet to Ashley." He handed it back to Dan, then hooked his thumbs in his pant pockets in one smooth motion. "It was a gift on her twentieth wedding anniversary."

"Do you know where we found this?" Greg exclaimed, unable to contain his excitement anymore, his words more of a statement than a question.

"I imagine you found it during your search of the Dismal Swamp," the mayor replied. To answer Greg's astonishment, he added, "I like to keep tabs on what goes on around here. After all, most of the refuge lies within my town's borders. And of course, the coroner called me after you told him about your new evidence on your way over here. All in all, I'd say you've done a good job so far. But then, you still need to get an autopsy to confirm your suspicion . . . of murder."

"Who said anything about murder?" Dan quickly countered. He didn't wish to reveal anything yet until he knew the mayor's motives.

"You're right, of course, Mr. Mayor," Greg pounced, before the mayor could challenge Dan. "It would have to be murder, if it wasn't an accident. We were just discussing the possibility of requesting an autopsy from Mr. Myrtle when you joined us."

"Yes, I heard." The mayor smiled. "I don't think you'll have any luck, even with your new evidence. Of course, you could get a Federal judge to order one," he added, glancing at Dan with wary eyes. The mayor's emphasis on the word *Federal* had dripped with disdain. "But forcing the issue might not be the best approach in a small town like this, where everyone knows everyone. I could have a talk with Jonathan and convince him of the wisdom of an autopsy. He'll look more kindly on hearing it from a friend," he said, emphasizing the last word, "than he would from a couple of representatives of the Federal government. We tend to look a little askew at outsiders telling us our business."

"So we've seen," Dan remarked, remembering the confrontation with the coroner. "Will Mr. Schmidt be willing to allow us to watch?" Dan asked. Greg didn't relish this prospect; it repelled him to think of Ashley Myrtle, such a beauty, being carved up like a Thanksgiving turkey. But in this case, it was part of his job.

"Leave everything to me." The mayor smiled, shook their hands, and turned away. "I'll have Ken call you when he's ready," Greeley called over his shoulder as he moved down the hall into the fading light. Then he paused. "And you will keep me informed of your investigation?" he asked. This was the price they would pay, Greg suspected, in exchange for the mayor's help.

Dan grimaced. "Well, it's a Federal investigation." But Greg didn't hesitate and appended, "But you'll be the first to know after we know anything." He waved.

"Excellent! Good day, gentlemen." The heels of the big man clicked and echoed on the worn ceramic floor, then faded.

Dan and Greg turned in the other direction toward the large arched doors.

Dan waited until they had left the building and were down the steps before he blurted, "What did you do that for?"

"I just said he'd be the first to know. I didn't say *when* he'd know it. Besides, we need his help."

"And of course, if it was murder, her husband is the prime suspect. Don't you think the mayor knows that? He'd like nothing more than to tarnish his main competition before the election. Why else do you think he's agreed to get us the autopsy?"

"I don't care why. I only hope we're right, or we'll have more than just egg on our faces," Greg murmured.

Chapter Fourteen

When Dan got the call, it was 11:30 P.M. He thanked the coroner, who only grunted in reply, and then called Greg. They met back at the coroner's office thirty minutes later. Ken Schmidt led them down to the morgue, where the body lay on a stainless steel table, under a green sheet.

"I don't suppose either one of you has ever been to a medical autopsy before?" he asked before uncovering Ashley Myrtle's body.

"Yes" and "No" were the simultaneous replies from Dan and Greg respectively.

"Well, for those of you who haven't seen one before, if you feel the need to lose your lunch, kindly leave the room beforehand," Schmidt announced. "And if you can't make it out of the room"—he pointed past the pair

119

of attentive men—"there's a basin behind you. Try not to miss. It's the janitor's night off."

Ken pulled off the sheet with one smooth motion and allowed it to flutter in the air for a moment before gathering it into a ball and handing it to a large young black man with cropped hair. He pulled on a headset with a small microphone and placed the recorder in his pocket after turning it on. He cleared his throat before he spoke.

"Subject is Ashley Myrtle, white female Caucasian, age forty-four years. Cause of death, unknown. This is a limited, noninvasive autopsy, in that no scalpels will be used and no entry wounds made." In response to Dan's puzzled glance, he added, "Husband's request."

"There are several abrasions on the fingertips, two nails on the right hand are broken and one pulled back from the cuticle, starting with the index finger and including the third and fourth digits. The left hand has one broken nail on the pinky," he said aloud into his headset.

"Typical defensive wounds, wouldn't you say?" Dan interrupted.

Schmidt gave him a glance that was not welcoming, but he did not speak.

The assistant wheeled a stand to the autopsy table with a machine on it—a fluid extractor, Schmidt explained—and plugged it into a wall socket with an extension cord. The coroner removed a coil and placed the tip, a small tube about one-half inch in diameter, into the woman's mouth. He pressed a switch, and the electric engine hummed. A harsh sound, a mixture of sucking and slurping as from the bottom of a glass with a straw, greeted their ears. It stopped suddenly however, and the coroner retrieved the end of the tube.

"Eh? What's this?" he asked, and he pulled a clump of mud from the end of the tube, large enough to block it. "That's rather odd." He set the clump aside on a small tray and replaced the tube. Several more particles of dirt and two more large clumps were sucked up in the next few minutes.

Ken Schmidt recorded their discovery on his headset, and Greg nodded at Dan when he caught the agent's attention. This confirmed what they had suspected, that Ashley's face had been held down in the mud. Greg examined the dirt as closely as he could without touching it, and Schmidt eyed him warily as Greg's nose threaten to bump into the tray. Greg was so close, he could detect the muddy scent, which was a mixture of something he could only conclude was water and peat moss mixed with sod.

"Hungry, are we? This isn't a diner," Ken announced, and Greg backed away from the table to stand next to Dan.

Dan whispered in his ear, "Do you always sniff the evidence?"

Greg didn't glance at him but scowled.

"Several pieces of dirt and mud were found in the mouth and esophagus. I am now recovering any fluid from the lungs," Ken said into the headset. He pushed the tube deeper down her throat and turned on the machine again. Greg watched as an ounce of two of liquid was pulled through the tube into a small collecting jar beneath the machine. The coroner then pulled the tube out and guided it back into her airway and into the other lung and repeated the procedure. Only a few drips of fluid were retrieved. After removing the tube, the coroner drew blood samples from the femoral artery in the leg. The blood had an unnatural appearance, thick and brownish, instead of the bright red color Greg had expected.

"These samples will be sent to our lab for analysis, but assuming they're clean, I think we can call this an accident," Ken said with a sigh but not without some satisfaction.

Greg lunged forward and began to speak but ran into the stiff, upraised arm of Dan, who cut him off with the words, "I'd like to examine the other side of the body."

"Eh?" Schmidt asked.

"The other side of the body," he repeated.

"Huh?" Ken said.

"The dead body," Dan emphasized. "Can we flip her over?"

The coroner shrugged his shoulders, as if he had no objection either way, and motioned to his assistant. The two men turned Ashley Myrtle over on the table, and both Dan and Greg approached for a closer look.

"See? Here, and here on the shoulder blades," Greg said, and pointed. Dan nodded. "I'd like some pictures of this, if you don't mind," Greg said.

Schmidt shrugged again and looked at his assistant. "Jim, can you get out the camera?"

Jim snapped a picture of the body, and Greg, unsatisfied with just one, asked to borrow it. He took several close-ups of each shoulder blade, which showed bruising and skin trauma.

"How do you explain that?" Dan challenged. "This was no accident! Look at those bruises! And the lack of water in her lungs!"

"I see the bruises. Doesn't mean they were inflicted by a perpetrator. She could have gotten those as she struggled for her life. She must have panicked toward the end," Schmidt asserted.

"Bruises on her back?" Greg asked as he handed Jim the camera. "Even you must find that unusual."

"Unusual but not unheard of," Schmidt countered. "Son," he said with a patronizing air, "when you've seen as many dead bodies as I have, in about thirty years or so you'll recognize that this is not so unusual. Every drowning is a tragedy, but it doesn't have to be a murder."

"So, you're not going to change the cause of death?" Greg asked with surprise.

"I'll let you know when the toxicology tests come in. Then you can read my final report. If there're any surprises, you'll be the first to know. Well, gentlemen, if there's nothing else, I've got work to do."

"I trust you'll include the photos with your report?" Dan asked as they headed for the door to leave.

Schmidt simply smiled and gave a salute, then turned

his attention back to the body. He and Jim were covering Ashley Myrtle back up with the green sheet as Greg and Dan exited.

Ken Schmidt waited until they had left the morgue and walked to a small sink to wash his hands, then dried them on a clean towel. The smell of vanilla wafted up to his nose—the result of the fragrant soap, which helped cover the odors of formaldehyde and body fluids. Jim had already left for his dinner break. When Ken heard the outer doors of the morgue close and was satisfied that the pair of investigators was gone, he turned and picked up his phone, dialing on the old rotary dial. The phone rang twice before he heard a click.

"Yeah, it's me," he began. "No, they just left. Looks like they were right. She didn't drown. Well, let's just say that someone probably helped her." He listened for a moment, then blurted, "No, I didn't tell them anything. As a matter of fact, I didn't change the preliminary cause of death. They weren't too satisfied with that. Well, they may be a couple of Yankees, but they're not fools." He listened for another few seconds. "They'll be asking a lot of questions, and they're pretty sharp, especially that kid. Yeah, he's not as dumb as he pretends to be. Good-bye, Mr. Mayor," he said before he hung up the phone. He lit a cigarette and glanced at Ashley. "What a waste," he said aloud. He took another drag and left the room.

Jim, his assistant, was just sitting down to eat when Ken came into the break room. He held a small brown bag.

"Cleaned and dressed, ready for the mortician, eh, Jim?" he said with a swagger as he swung into the seat opposite his assistant. He dangled the brown bag and shook it once. "My missus made some fine blueberry muffins. Care for a taste?"

"Yes, sir," Jim said through a mouthful of sandwich.

Ken eagerly openly the bag and placed two muffins on the paper towels that Jim had spread on the table in the dinnertime ritual they had practiced for years.

Ken leaned back in his chair. "Forgot to cut 'em," he said, and an impish grin flickered across his face. He extended an index finger into the air, as though struck by inspiration.

"Ah, I know," he said suddenly, and he looked around while he rubbed his hands on his belly. "Where's my bread knife?" he asked.

The next sound was a loud, food-clogged cough from Jim, followed by a gut-felt peal of laughter from the coroner.

"I can't believe he wouldn't admit it!" Greg said in exasperation as they drove away from the municipal building. He cracked his knuckles loudly and shook his head in disgust.

Dan eyed him while sporting a wry smile. "C'mon!" he badgered Greg. "You didn't really think that two-bit surgeon was going to take the word of a twenty-something Yankee transplant from Wilkes-Barre, Pennsylvania, did you? You're gonna need more than just a few facts to win these people over. Maybe you should practice your drawl—you know, maybe listen to a few Elvis interviews, get that tone down right." Dan cleared his throat and mimicked the King. "Uh, Mr. Coroner, sir. Thankyouverymuch!" he drawled. Greg did not smile in return. He was silent for a few moments.

"Well, he did admit that the bruises were unusual."

"Uh-huh."

"So, we should have enough to keep investigating."

"Maybe."

"Maybe? Whadya mean *maybe*?"

"Okay, okay," Dan demurred, and he held up a hand. "I'll keep my investigation open. How about you? Do you want to tag along and share information, or is the Fish and Wildlife department out of the picture at this point?"

"I have to call my boss. He's in Florida, and, frankly, I was hoping to avoid it."

"Florida? Shouldn't he be here? Do you mean he doesn't even know?" Dan said with surprise.

"His mom's dying. I didn't want to bother him. So far as he knows, it's just an accidental drowning of some tourist. He doesn't know who yet."

"Does that matter? I mean, a woman's dead in his domain. Does it really matter who she was?"

"My boss knows all the local politicians. I remember the councilman asking me where Floyd was when all this started, as if I couldn't wipe my nose without Floyd showing me how."

"I see," Dan said thoughtfully. "Well, if you want to

stay on board, I'll let you tag along on *my* investigation," he emphasized.

The statement brought a frown to Greg's face. "I'll call my boss first thing in the morning," he said.

Chapter Fifteen

It was past 2:00 A.M. when Greg cracked open the front door and wiggled his key out of the stiff lock, the tumblers catching on the worn metal. He crept into the kitchen and opened the refrigerator. The memory of last night's lasagna caused a rumble to erupt from the pit of his stomach. His hand was just about to latch onto the baking dish behind the mayonnaise jar when the entire kitchen exploded in light.

"Greg! I could make you something," a voice called out.

"It's okay, Ma. I'm just eating some leftovers. Did I wake you?"

A short, stout woman stood in the doorway leading from the dining room. A shaggy robe hung on her shoulders and was tied around her waist with a cloth belt that didn't match the robe. She shuffled, rather than walked, to the table, and reached out with a gnarled hand whose fingers worked as one to clutch a chair. Greg rushed to assist her as she hung her cane over the chair back. He ushered her into the seat, and she sat down heavily and drew a deep breath.

"What are you doing up?" Greg asked.

"I heard you come in," she said. "I thought you might want something to eat. How'd it go at the coroner?"

"Well, I wasn't looking forward to it, but I didn't faint, if that's what you mean."

"Good grief!" Debbie Parnell cried. "You had to watch that? What for?"

"Ma, it's my job. I don't expect you to understand," Greg said with exasperation.

"Is she the one you found in the swamp? I thought she drowned."

"I had my doubts about that from the start," Greg said as he cut a thick slice of lasagna and placed it on a plate in the microwave.

"Well, if she didn't drown, how'd she die?"

Greg grimaced, an action that produced a sharp intake of breath from his mother.

"Oh, my God! Greg, you'd better be careful!"

"I always am, Mother," he said impatiently, not for the first time.

"I'm serious. Chasing poachers was one thing, but this!"

"That's why they give us guns, Ma," he said with some annoyance. "Besides, chasing poachers is a lot more dangerous."

Debbie didn't say anything, but Greg heard a quick guffaw in response. The microwave bell sounded, and Greg placed his plate on the kitchen table. "Want some tea?" he asked. At a negative nod from his mother, he turned his attention hungrily to his food.

"I'm going to bed, unless you need something."

"I'm fine, Ma. Good night."

He watched as Debbie gripped a small cane with her swollen hands and hobbled out of the kitchen. Her hands were getting worse, and there didn't seem to be anything he could do about it. The newest drugs, genetically engineered, were getting rave reviews in clinical trials, but the price he had heard quoted would put them far out of reach for his mom.

But at the moment he had more pressing matters to attend to. One of them, his hunger, was being taken care of. The other, a phone call to Floyd, the refuge manager, would have to wait a few more hours.

He finished his food and set his plate in the sink before heading off to bed. He plopped onto his unmade bed and kicked the blanket down to the foot. Without air-conditioning, a covering was a waste of time, and although the night was cool, Greg tossed and turned for what seemed like hours.

Sooner than he'd hoped, the radio alarm sounded, announcing what, according to the DJ, was the beginning of a glorious day. He stumbled into the living room and muttered his doubts. He picked up the phone, retrieved a slip of paper from his wallet, and dialed a number. He was beginning to think that perhaps 8:00 A.M. was too early for this when a voice answered after the sixth ring.

"Culpeppers' " was all it said.

"Hello? Is Mr. Floyd Culpepper there?" Greg asked sleepily.

"This is he. Greg? Is that you?" the voice returned.

Greg shot to attention as he realized he was speaking to his boss. "Uh, yes, sir. Sorry to call you so early, but I couldn't wait any longer," he explained.

"This wouldn't have anything to do with Ashley Myrtle's death, would it?"

Stunned, Greg affirmed that suspicion. "How did you know?"

"Small-town news. Everybody knows everybody's business, even here in Florida. Why don't you give me your side of it?" he said. Unaware that there was more than one side from which to tell what had happened, Greg explained the finding of the body and his suspicions about the cause of death. He told Floyd of his search for the crime scene and the help he'd received from Dan Brennan, and he concluded with the abbreviated autopsy they had been able to extract from an unwilling array of locals.

Floyd listened silently, with only an occasional murmur.

"That sounds about right, although nowhere near the story I got from Jonathan Myrtle. Of course, a distraught husband is apt to exaggerate a bit," Floyd said.

"He called you?" Greg asked with surprise.

"Like I said, small towns. And he made his position

clear in no uncertain terms. He wants us out of the picture, and I can't say I blame him. Not that I doubt you, but this seems a bit out of our jurisdiction."

"Yes, sir," Greg conceded, and his heart sank. "We do have some evidence out with our forensics lab in Oregon. I wanted to verify some fauna that was found on the body."

"That's fine. Now, you mentioned this FBI agent, Dan something?"

"Brennan, sir."

"Does he have a bead on this?" Floyd asked.

"Well, he's opened a file, and he's also convinced it was murder."

"Good. We can drop it into his lap, exit the case, and keep our good relations with the local public officials. After all, we have to work with them."

"I understand."

"Besides, you can still check on the case from time to time. But let the Feds handle this, okay?"

"Yes, sir."

"And, Greg?"

"Yes, sir?"

"You can call me Floyd. I'm not that formal."

"Yes, sir. I mean, Floyd."

"I guess you haven't been too bored in our little neck of the woods, have you?"

"Um, not at all. I wouldn't want to find a body every day, but I like to keep my skills sharp. How's your mom, by the way?"

"Still hanging in there. My sister got in just today,

thank goodness. The whole family's here now. At least she'll have that."

"Well, don't worry about anything here. I'll take care of everything."

"Good. That's a relief. You know, I thought I might actually have to come back up, but after talking to you, I feel better about the whole thing. Although it makes me a little nervous, since I'm the refuge manager. It's still my responsibility if things go wrong."

"I won't let you down, Floyd," Greg said firmly.

"That's all I needed to hear. Thanks, Greg. Keep me informed if anything else happens," Floyd said.

Greg hung up and heard noises from the kitchen. He walked in to find his mother cooking bacon and making a pot of coffee. She turned from the stove to smile at Greg as he sat down.

"Everything okay with your boss?" she asked softly.

"Yeah, everything's fine," Greg said.

"I couldn't help overhearing. It sounded as if you were in trouble, the way you were talking."

"No, no trouble," he said, and he accepted the cup of coffee she placed before him. He added sugar and milk, stirred it, and took a deep sip before he continued. "Everything's fine, except I have to give the case to the FBI," he said.

"Oh, good. I thought it might be something bad."

"Ma," Greg said loudly, and gained her attention. "It is bad. I wanted to work this case."

"You did? Oh, then, that's bad. Maybe you'll get to work the next one. How many eggs do you want?"

Greg nearly laughed at her ability to change the subject and focus on something more immediate, like breakfast. "I'll take three," he said.

"Over easy?"

"Yes, thanks," he replied.

"Don't mention it. That's what mothers are for."

Chapter Sixteen

By the time Greg got to the refuge headquarters, it was almost 11:00 A.M. He didn't think anyone would miss him, but as he walked in, Cindy placed a hand over the mouthpiece of the phone, whispered something, and handed him a pink message slip and a report from Brad.

He walked into the main office. The message was from Floyd, asking Greg to call him in Florida. He thought it might have been an old message, but it was dated today, in fact, and was less than an hour old. Not sure what to make of it, he glanced out to see that Cindy was still on the phone.

The other paper was Brad's report on the gate at Washington Ditch. It appeared that someone had tried to file through the combination lock. A bird-watcher approaching the gate had observed a man in a white truck drive away in some haste. There was no detailed description, and Brad had only been able to determine that the suspect was a white male. Brad concluded that the man had exited the refuge through the Jericho Ditch, which was open that day. The lock had only minor damage, apparently from a metal file, but Brad noted that he would buy another lock and replace it.

Greg set the report down and waited for the sound of Cindy hanging up the phone. He studied the large map of the refuge that Floyd kept pinned to the wall and monitored the front reception area, where Cindy was. He was eager to return Floyd's call as soon as possible. He was looking at the map when he heard footsteps and turned to see Dan Brennan standing in the doorway.

"Let's go, Bucko, time's a-wasting," he said, and he tossed a set of keys into the air and caught them.

"Forget it. I'm off the case."

"Really?" Dan said, as if he didn't believe him.

"Are you taunting me? Because I'm not in the mood."

Dan placed a hand over his heart. "Would I do that to you?" he asked.

Greg wanted to laugh at this act, but more than that, he wanted to be taken seriously. So he kept a serious look on his face.

"Uh, have you gotten a phone call in the last hour or so, or am I just imagining this trip?" Dan asked. He took a seat in a chair across from Greg.

Just then, Cindy walked into the office. "Floyd called. He's wants you to call him. Sorry I was on the phone, but I'm off now," she explained. "Did you tell him?" she asked Dan, looking at the FBI agent.

"Tell me what?" Greg asked a little too loudly. He was still tired from the restless night he'd spent, disappointed with his removal from the murder investigation, and wondering, not for the first time, how many days it was until retirement.

He wasn't helping his mom on his salary, his first few days at this job were turning into a disaster, and the future looked bleak. After the initial blinding success of his undercover work, he'd seemed to run into obstacles with every decision he'd made.

Had he made a mistake coming here? Had he peaked already? Suddenly retirement seemed a very long way off.

He held his head in his hands and suddenly became aware of a deafening silence. He looked up to find Cindy and Dan staring at him as if he had two heads. He picked up the phone and began to dial. "I'll call him," he said softly.

Cindy nodded and smiled. Dan stretched his arms and yawned as though bored.

Cindy left the office to assist a visitor who had just entered the refuge office. This time Floyd answered on the second ring.

"Greg?"

"Yes. Cindy said you wanted to talk to me?"

"Yeah. Looks like the FBI can't do without you. Remember that agent who was investigating the case? Well, his supervisor called me and asked if they could borrow one of our people, seeing as how the case hinged on quite a bit of evidence found in the refuge. Since we've got the technical expertise in the wild, I agreed, and since you're already involved with it, seems like you're the natural choice."

"Yes, sir," Greg said, forgetting the informality he had promised to use.

"So, give this guy, Dan Brennan, your full cooperation. We're strictly advisors on this, but of course, use your discretion. If you think something needs doing and it's not getting done, advise the agent."

"I understand, Floyd."

"Good. Guess you're back on the case. Good luck," he said warmly.

Greg thanked him and put down the receiver. He looked up and found Dan studying him intently. Greg immediately suppressed his smile and attempted to replace it with a serious expression.

"Uh, he said you needed our help with this case, so he wanted to know if I could assist the Bureau—if I have the time, that is," Greg said with as much seriousness he could muster.

"Uh-huh," Dan said. "So, do you?"

"Do I what?"

"Have the time to help us? Or do you have to rescue Bambi from a poacher or something?"

Greg looked in an appointment book that was lying on the desk and muttered, "Well, I guess I can spare the time." He looked up to see Dan headed for the door. "I'll be in the car," he called over his shoulder.

Greg headed out after him and waved to Cindy as he departed.

"Where to?" he asked as Dan pulled out of the parking lot.

"The Chesapeake Conservancy, out on Military Highway," Dan said. "I want to go to Ashley Myrtle's office, talk to the people who saw her last. According to your report, she left for the swamp about one P.M. on Tuesday. You guys found her Wednesday around noon. We want to account for everyone's movements, see if anyone saw her leave, that sort of thing."

"I'd also like to know how the truck got back to the office without her. She must have been with someone," Greg said.

"And I figure that someone drove."

"Well, we'll find out soon enough. Turn right here," Greg said.

Dan turned off White Marsh Road onto George Washington Road, heading north, and followed it to Route 13. After twenty minutes, they slowed, and Dan pulled into a ranch-style, modern-looking building near the intersection of Military Highway and Battlefield Boulevard. The parking lot held several cars, and a large sign out front displayed the silhouette of a pelican-in-flight with the words CHESAPEAKE CONSERVANCY printed below in light-blue lettering.

They walked up to the entrance and through the front door to a small reception desk, where a woman with dirty-blond hair was hanging up the phone. She wore a blue dress and wire-rimmed glasses.

"Can I help you?" she asked pleasantly.

Her smile faded when Dan showed her his badge and ID. "This is about Ashley, isn't it?" she guessed, and Dan nodded.

He turned and gestured to Greg. "This is Greg Parnell, special agent with the Fish and Wildlife Service. Can we have a list of the people who were working here Tuesday, in the afternoon? We're going to need to interview them."

"Sure. To start with, I was working that afternoon."

"And you are?" Dan began, pen poised above a notebook he pulled from his jacket.

"Pam Sutherland. I'm the receptionist, assistant, gopher, what have you."

"Anyone else working here that day?" Dan continued.

"Uh, Carol, the office manager, down the hall. Earl, I think, and well, that's it. Normally the volunteers don't work on Tuesday. That's a staff day, to catch up on paperwork. Oh, and Mary Bailey was in. She's in charge of the newsletter and fund-raising, but she left by noon. She usually only works in the morning."

Dan finished writing and noticed that Greg was looking at the pictures on the reception area wall. He tried to catch his eye but failed.

"Um, is there an office we can use?" Dan asked.

"Down the hall, past Ashley's office, there's a conference room at the end on the right."

"Okay. We'll talk to Carol and Earl, and then call you, if that's all right."

"Sure. But Earl's not here. He's out, but he should be back soon."

"That's fine. I'll call you in when we need to talk to you."

Dan headed down the hall, followed by Greg.

"I was listening," he said in response to a look of irritation from Dan. They paused at Carol's office, where Dan introduced himself and asked her to step into the conference room. They proceeded in while she shut down her computer and Dan grabbed Greg's attention.

"I'll ask the questions, but if you want to know something I'm not leading to, jump in after catching my eye. How's that suit you?"

"That's fine," Greg said. They sat down, and Dan scanned the walls. "There's a picture on that wall, if you're bored," he said and pointed to a reproduction of Edvard Munch's *The Scream*. Greg didn't have time to respond, as Carol entered the room.

Dan and Greg shook hands with her as the introductions were repeated. From experience or upbringing, both men rose and waited for Carol to take a seat before returning to their own. She was about thirty years old, Greg guessed from the stylish cut that framed her face with brown hair. She wore a white blouse with a denim skirt. A gold necklace hung from her neck; it matched a gold bracelet on her right hand.

"First, we just wanted to say how sorry we are about Mrs. Myrtle's death and extend our condolences," Dan began. Greg nodded his assent but didn't speak.

"Thank you," Carol replied, and she adjusted the bracelet, which had inched toward her forearm, back onto her wrist. She rested her hands in front of her on the conference table.

"Second, just to inform you, we're investigating Mrs. Myrtle's death strictly as a formality. The preliminary results show that she most likely drowned, but we have to keep an open mind until we have all the facts."

"I understand," she said hesitantly.

"We just want to get an idea of her movements on the day she disappeared, on Tuesday. You were here that day?" Dan asked.

"That's right," Carol began, and she brought her hands together, playing with her bracelet. "I usually work from nine to twelve, but we had a lot of work to catch up on, so I stayed until one-thirty."

"And what time did Ashley leave for the refuge?"

Carol squinted, as though she was trying to recall the exact time. She looked at Dan and then Greg and shook her head. "To tell you the truth, I'm not really sure. I think it was about twelve o'clock or a little before."

"That's fine," Dan said with a smile. "We're actually more interested in how she went to the refuge. Did you see who she left with?"

"No, I'm afraid not. You see, I was in my office doing our quarterly budget, and I remember hearing her say that she was leaving, but that's about all," she confessed. Her bracelet clinked against the engagement ring on her left hand.

"Well, when you left, did you see her car?" Dan asked.

"Yes," Carol began. "But I just assumed she'd gone with someone."

"Anyone else here when you left?"

"Well, Earl's office door was closed, so he must have left before noon. Uh, Pam was here. She's usually the last to leave, unless Ashley's still here." She suddenly put a hand to her mouth, and Greg thought he discerned a gasp from her throat.

Dan sat up and stopped writing and looked as though he were about to ask her something. After a few seconds, he did. "Are you all right?"

Carol nodded, but her hand still covered her mouth as though suppressing some deep emotional pain. She was silent for several seconds, a time frame that seemed like an eternity in the quiet of the large conference room.

Finally, she spoke. "I just remembered. Today was her twenty-fifth wedding anniversary." After a few moments, she apologized and relaxed.

"So, it was just Pam here when you left?"

"Yes." And then she paused for a moment. "I thought there was another car in the parking lot." She shook her head after some thought. "No, I must be wrong."

"Are you sure?" Greg asked, bolting upright in his chair, where he'd been listening in a relaxed pose. The change was so sudden that Dan and Carol both appeared startled.

"No. I mean, I'm pretty sure," Carol said. "I mean, I

really don't remember for sure," she admitted. "We have a number of volunteers who work on different days, and we get visitors. Who can remember from one day to the next? Is it important?" she asked apprehensively.

"No, not really," Greg said, and he smiled at her.

"Okay, well, that's all we need for now," Dan said. They all stood up, and Dan asked, "Could you cover the front desk and have Pam step in here?" Carol nodded and turned toward the door.

"I almost forgot," Greg said, and he tugged at his ear.

Carol and Dan turned and paused.

"What exactly did Ashley do around here, anyway?" Greg asked.

Carol thought for a moment. "She was the director, so she pretty much led the organization," she replied. She turned again to leave.

"What does that mean, exactly?" Greg continued.

Carol paused and seemed about to speak, but she hesitated. Her face wore a puzzled expression.

"What I mean is, what was it like, day to day? For instance, did she just give people their marching orders, and that was that? Did she sit in her office and rule the roost?" Greg speculated aloud.

"Oh, no. Nothing like that," Carol said, energized with the memory of her former leader. "She wasn't afraid to get her feet wet, in a manner of speaking. When we had a Clean the Bay Day about three months ago, she was the first one in the water, pulling old tires and garbage out of Lynnhaven Creek."

"I remember that campaign," Greg said with a smile.

"So she wasn't afraid to get in and work with the grunts, so to speak?"

"Not at all. In fact, we all asked her to wear a life preserver when we were cleaning the river, but she refused. She didn't think it would look good in the newspaper. She wanted good publicity for the group."

"So she was the only one without a vest?" Dan asked.

"Actually, she was the only one who needed one in shallow water," Carol explained.

"Why's that?" Dan asked with sudden interest.

Greg was already sitting down, for he knew what was next. He shook his head in dismay.

"She couldn't swim," Carol replied.

"Couldn't swim? Really?" Dan asked, and he shot a look at Greg. "Well, imagine that."

"Honest. We urged her to take lessons at the YMCA, but she never had the time. That what makes this tragedy so senseless. If she could swim, she'd still be here, wouldn't she?"

Dan nodded, then gazed at Greg. "Anything else?" Greg simply waved, and Dan signaled to Carol that she could leave.

"Nice try," Dan said.

"I was hoping against hope," Greg explained. His head was still bowed in discouragement. "We still have a case, though," he murmured.

"We have a theory," Dan countered. "And unless we come up with more, that's all it is." He slapped his notebook onto the conference table with disgust.

A moment later Pam knocked timidly on the door of

the conference room and entered. Dan smiled and pointed to a chair. She made herself comfortable and offered them some refreshments, which they turned down.

"I don't mind telling you, I was a little apprehensive when you showed me that badge," she said with a smile. "After what happened, I thought maybe—" Pam said, but she left her sentence unfinished.

Dan simply nodded and smiled, to set her at ease. But Greg seized the opportunity. "Maybe, what?"

"Huh?" Pam blurted, and she turned to look at Greg. Her eyes revealed that she hadn't expected a reply and that she might now be sorry.

"What did you think?" Greg elaborated. His folded his arms and leaned forward to concentrate on her response.

She was silent for a moment. She looked to Dan for guidance, which suddenly wasn't there, and turned to look at Greg again. Her face began to redden, just slightly, but a definite hue formed.

"Well, I . . ." she began, and she rubbed her arms as though fending off a chill. "I guess, I thought, maybe, like . . . she'd been killed, or something."

Chapter Seventeen

"Interesting that you should say that," Dan said. He looked at his notes and flipped a couple of pages as though searching for some information. He paused and merely added, "Uh-huh."

"What does that mean? Does that mean she was killed, that she didn't drown like the paper said?" Pam asked, seizing on Dan's actions.

"Let's just say that you're not the first person to speculate on that," Greg said. "We can't elaborate further."

"But we'd like to know why you think that's a possibility," Dan said.

Between the two of them, Pam's head bobbled back and forth as they tried to catch her off guard. "Well, it's probably nothing," she said. "But she did get a couple of harassing phone calls."

147

Dan sat up and began to jot in his notebook. "When was this?"

"Uh, about two weeks ago, I think."

"Did she report it?" Greg asked.

"No. Ashley just dismissed them as crank calls."

"What time of day did they come through?" Dan asked.

"Usually in the morning, around ten o'clock or so."

"I see," Dan said. "Did she mention if she knew who it was, recognize the voice, anything like that?"

"No, she just thought they were some jerks who were angry about her report."

Both men looked up at the same time, looked at each other and then at Pam.

"What report?" Greg asked.

"The wetlands report she was working on. It was her biggest project ever. Didn't Carol mention it? She's the one you should really talk to about it."

"Why don't you tell us what you know about it?" Dan suggested.

"Um, not much, really. It was pretty hush-hush around the office. She had a little help on it from Earl, but most of it she was doing herself." She looked uncomfortable but refused Dan's offer of a short break.

"Any particular reason for the secrecy?" Dan asked. He was trying to concentrate on the interview, but he kept catching glimpses of Greg as he moved around the room and looked out the window.

Pam shrugged her shoulders and said, "I'm just a receptionist."

"Don't be afraid to let us know what you think," Greg said. He sensed some hesitancy on Pam's part. "The parking lot's empty. There's no one here but us."

With a sly smile, Dan understood his interest in the window.

Pam nodded. She leaned forward to speak, as though someone might still be eavesdropping. "It's just that some people wanted the report to reflect their viewpoint, and others wanted another viewpoint. We're trying to clean up the bay, so Ashley was determined to be honest and say what had to be done. I'm sure some of the developers were worried that it would cut back on some of their projects."

"You mean, prevent them from building at the water's edge?" Greg asked.

"That's right," Pam confirmed.

"Hardly seems like a big deal. I mean, people will still build houses, right?" Dan asked.

Greg turned to Dan and explained. "There's a big push to restrict building within two hundred feet of the Chesapeake Bay watershed. That would prevent houses from being built not only on the bay itself but along any tributary, creek, or river that feeds into the bay, which means that practically every waterfront property could be off limits for building in the southeastern Virginia region. Millions of dollars are at stake, not to mention hundreds of jobs and the tax revenue. Do you know what waterfront property goes for around here?"

Dan grunted. "I priced some houses along the Elizabeth River in Suffolk. It's a pretty penny, that's for sure."

"And not just waterfront property. A lot of people want to restrict building on nontidal wetlands," Greg added. "They're vital to the ecosystem in coastal areas like this, because they act like a huge sponge, soaking up water during heavy storms and filtering it of pollutants. The refuge is covered with them, and they help control flooding and provide cover for wildlife. The legislature has been under a lot of pressure to impose restrictions on destroying them."

"And her report, what does it say about this?" Dan asked Pam.

"I'm not really sure, but the points you made," she said, looking at Greg, "are all valid. I'm sure she would have recommended some sort of restrictions on development in several areas. The governor has already publicly announced that he would endorse her findings."

"Our governor?" Greg asked with surprise. "She must pull a lot of weight."

"She and the governor are old friends," Pam explained.

"Why don't we see what it says for ourselves?" Greg said suddenly. Dan nodded. "Do you have a key to her office?"

Pam led them out of the conference room and opened Ashley's locked office. "Is this okay? I mean, should you have a warrant, or something?"

"As long as you give us permission, we don't need a warrant," Dan explained. Besides, we're not looking for evidence of a crime *by* Ashley. We're looking for evidence of a crime against her."

"Oh. I guess that's all right, then," she said, and she

stepped aside as the two men entered. "Is there any-thing in particular you're looking for?" she asked.

"How about an appointment book or address book?" Dan suggested. On the desk, he spied a large black folder with spiral binding.

"This looks promising," he said, and he opened the book, flipped a couple of pages, and stopped. He pulled out his notebook and pen as Greg looked on.

"This is interesting. Tuesday, B. Meyers, noon," he said aloud as he jotted down the entry. "Any idea who that might be?"

"Uh, that would be Bill Meyers. He's a friend of the family," Pam reassured him. "I've heard Ashley mention him a number of times."

"The day she disappeared?" Greg added.

"I'm sure it's nothing, but we'll need to check him out, if only to eliminate him," Dan reassured her. Greg noted a number just below the man's name: *015-26.*

"What's that?" he asked, pointing it out to Dan.

Dan glanced at Pam, who shook her head in igno-rance. "You use combination locks, don't you? Maybe it's part of the combination to a gate, or a security code of some sort?" he asked, and he looked at Greg.

"Maybe," Greg confessed. "I haven't memorized all the combinations. We've got six gates entering the refuge. I'll check that out."

Dan continued to leaf back through the pages of the appointment book and pointed to one or two entries. "The guy who works here?" he asked.

"Um, they have weekly meetings about the report or

other business. They worked on a lot of projects to-gether," she explained.

"How about the report itself? Would it be on her computer?" Dan asked, looking for the power button.

"I'm afraid I'm going to have to let Carol handle that one," Pam said, and she stepped between Dan and the desk. "I'm not sure I should be handing that out, espe-cially as so many people are waiting for it."

"You mean, the governor?"

"Especially the governor," she said.

"You have anything to ask?" Dan queried.

Greg was staring at a picture hanging on the wall. It was from a newspaper article, and it showed Ashley shaking hands with the mayor of Great Bridge at the water's edge of Lynnhaven Creek. Behind her, a tall man with a shaggy brown beard, wearing a flannel shirt, jeans, and hip-wader boots was beaming as he looked at her. Additional members of the group stood off to the side, some looking at the camera, others, in-cluding Pam, with their eyes fixed on Ashley. Greg was reading the text and looking at the photo, but not at Ashley. He was more interested in one of the others.

"Who is this man?" Greg asked, pointing to the pic-ture.

"That's Earl Thompson," Pam replied.

He turned to find her standing stiffly across the desk from him, her arms folded.

"He must have been very proud," he began, and then paused.

"Of her?" Pam asked, sounding confused.

"No, I mean, to be involved with the cleanup," he corrected her.

"Oh, that. Why, of course," she said, and Greg detected a slight sigh of relief. "He was very proud to be involved. I mean, the Conservancy is his whole life," she explained with some animation. Her hands moved through the air as she spoke.

"Was he here on Tuesday?" Greg asked.

Pam hesitated. "Yes, he was," she said slowly.

"And what time did he leave?"

"I'm not really sure. I left just after two, and his truck wasn't here, so I assumed he had left sometime earlier."

"Not sure? Wouldn't you have seen him leave, since you work at the reception desk?"

"Not necessarily. You see, he usually parks in the back and leaves by that door, in case his clothes are soiled from fieldwork. His research takes him into some pretty muddy backwaters. We have a tile floor back there that's easy to clean up."

"Well, I think we'll need to talk to Earl. Do you happen to know when he'll be back?" Dan inquired.

"Who wants to know?" a booming voice demanded.

Greg and Dan looked toward the doorway and saw that it was filled by an enormous man with a thick brown beard and a Norfolk Tides baseball cap. He did not look pleased to see them.

Chapter Eighteen

"Earl Thompson, I presume?" Greg inquired with a just a dash of humor.

"Who wants to know?" the man again demanded as he stepped into the office. "This office should be closed," he said, looking at Pam.

Before she could respond, Dan pulled his ID and showed it to him.

Earl's reaction was swift and grim. "So, she was murdered," he said. "I knew it!"

"How so?" Greg asked, and he stepped toward the man who towered over him by three inches and probably outweighed him by fifty pounds.

"Let's go into the conference room to discuss this," Dan said, and he tried to wave everyone out of the office, which now felt tight and cramped with so many people in it.

"There's nothing to discuss," Earl said loudly to Dan. Then he turned to answer Greg. "I just knew, that's all. There was no reason for her to drown—she was afraid of deep water. Why don't you find whoever killed her? What are you doing here?" he demanded.

"Trying to find out what happened," Greg explained.

"Can we discuss this outside?" Dan said with irritation. He placed a hand on the shoulder of the large man, and it brought an immediate response.

Earl pulled away from the agent's guiding hand and stepped up to him, placing his mouth inches away from the agent's face. "I don't need to discuss this. You need to get your act together and find Ashley's killer! Or is that too much to expect from one of Hoover's finest?"

Dan pushed his chest into the torso of the larger man and prepared to challenge him, but Greg intervened.

"C'mon, we don't have time for this. Let's review what we have," he urged Dan. Dan followed him reluctantly out the door and down the hall toward the conference room, keeping an eye on Earl, who returned his stare with an icy glare.

Dan finally turned his attention to Greg and gave him a quizzical look. Greg shook his head and then said loudly as they sat at the conference table, "We don't need Thompson's information anyway." Greg could see Earl's shadow in the hallway. The big man was just out of sight but listening.

"So, what have we got? She left here—what—about

two?" Greg asked, and he motioned for Dan to agree with him.

"Uh, yeah. That's right," Dan concurred, and he opened his notebook, but not before giving Greg a funny look.

"That is not right!" Earl said as he burst into the room from his listening post in the hallway.

Dan had just enough time to see Greg's smile disappear as he looked at Earl with a more serious expression.

"Well, that's not what we've concluded," Greg said in an official tone. He leaned back in his chair.

Earl grabbed a chair with a bearlike paw and swung it around, plopped into it heavily, and drew his elbows up onto the table. His hairy arms, bronzed from countless hours working outdoors, framed an animated face that danced with emotion as he spoke.

"She left here at eleven-thirty."

"Why should we believe you?" Greg asked.

"I was here!" Earl exploded. "Don't you think I know what I saw?"

"Let's say, for the moment, we believe you," Greg said. He quickly held up a hand to interrupt what promised to be another slew of choice words from Earl, who was leaning forward, his hands turning white from his grip on the edge of the mahogany table. "What happened, exactly?"

"I know what time it was, because she asked to borrow my truck. She had told me before about her trip to the Dismal Swamp. I even volunteered to go with her, but she said that it wouldn't be necessary, because she wouldn't be alone. Now I see I should have gone with her."

"Why's that?" Dan asked.

"Because she's dead!" Earl announced. He ran a hand through his hair and placed his cap on the table. "Sorry. I get a little excited sometimes."

"Hmm, I hadn't noticed," Greg deadpanned. "So, it was eleven-thirty? Not to beat a dead horse, but you're sure?"

"Yes. I was about to eat my lunch, when she came in and asked for the keys. I usually eat then, unless I'm in the field. I gave her the keys, and a Post-it with the combination to the Jericho gate lock. I'm the only one who knows it by heart," he said. "Sometimes I think this place would fall apart without me," he added, explaining his last remark. He suddenly slammed a fist into the table. "I should have insisted on going," he muttered.

Greg glanced over at Dan, who faintly shrugged. Greg thought this demonstration was a little too neat to be spontaneous.

"And when did you leave for the day?" Greg asked.

"Me?" Earl asked with some surprise. "Why?" He looked back and forth at both men.

"It's standard to ask these sorts of questions," Dan reassured him.

"I left around three, or so. I only live about a mile away, so I just walked," he finally said.

Greg studied Earl with a casual air and kept his chin in the palm of one hand, elbow rested on the table but eyes watchful of each muscle movement in Earl's frame, every change in facial expression. Something was wrong with Earl's response.

"So, you were the last to leave?" Greg asked.

"That's right," Earl said defensively.

"You always work behind closed doors?" Dan asked.

"What's that supposed to mean?" Earl asked, turning to face what he saw as an accusation.

"Do you normally work behind a closed door? I thought this was one big happy family," Dan said.

"Sometimes, when I don't want to be disturbed," Earl responded.

"Carol said your door was shut when she left at one-thirty," Greg added, and the remark brought Earl's attention back to him. "She assumed you were gone," Greg continued.

"Oh, that. I was working on the wetlands report for Ashley. We're the only ones who are supposed to see it until it's released. It's very important to the future of the Chesapeake Bay."

"Ashley let you work on that?" Greg said with a little surprise in his voice. "That's not what we heard."

"What did you hear?" Earl asked, the start of an accusation in his tone.

"You tell me," Greg countered.

Earl stood and walked to the door, shut it, and returned to his seat.

"Look," Earl said, spreading his enormous hands on the table, "there's a lot that goes on here that the others don't know about. Ashley knew she could trust me, and I did most of the fieldwork for this report. She kept it close to the vest, because she didn't want nosy people prying information out of her. She also told people I wasn't involved so they'd leave me alone and wouldn't pepper me with questions. That's all. But it was our report," he explained.

"I see," Greg said, leaning back. "So you and she, you were pretty close?"

"Like I said, there was a lot that went on that people didn't know about and didn't have to know. We shared a certain . . . well, let's just say we were very close," he said, gazing into space.

"Were you sleeping with her?" Dan asked suddenly.

Earl made a face as though he smelled something unpleasant. "Naw, it wasn't like that. It would have developed into something more eventually. But we weren't at that stage. If you want to look for suspects, look at that husband of hers. She was getting ready to leave him, you know."

"How did you know that?" Greg asked.

"Like I said, we shared a lot, the two of us. She was going to divorce him. She filed the papers just a few days ago—I think the day before she disappeared, as a matter of fact," he stated. "I can't believe she's gone," he added, almost to himself.

There was a pause in the conversation while each man collected his thoughts. Finally Dan said, "We're going to need a copy of that report."

"You can't have it," Earl quickly replied.

"Why not?"

"It's confidential."

"We're investigating a woman's death, and, from what you've told us, she was a friend of yours. Don't you want to help us here?" Dan asked.

"Sure, but the report has nothing to do with that. Besides, I told you, it's very important to the Bay's future. It has to be given to the governor when it's done."

"When will that be?" Greg asked.

Earl shook his head. "I don't know. We were hoping to finish it in another week or so, but now it may be a little while longer. But it's due May first, about six weeks from now. When I find . . . when I find the time to finish it, I'll give you a copy, after the governor gets one first."

"Look, we're certainly not going to broadcast it. We just want to look through it, see what she was working on," Dan explained. "And, despite your assurances, it may be more important than you think."

Earl stood and looked at his watch. "I told you what we were working on. I'm sorry, but I can't help you anymore. You'll have to wait. Now, if you'll excuse me, gentlemen, I have work to do."

"If you think of anything else, would you call me?" Dan asked, extending his business card. Earl snatched the card as he headed for the door. "Sure thing," he mumbled.

It was hard to believe anyone so large could move so quickly, but a moment later he was gone, leaving the two men alone in the conference room. Dan shook and scratched his head but was speechless.

"Did you just feel a breeze?" Greg asked.

"More like a hurricane. Let's get out of here," Dan quipped.

Chapter Nineteen

Greg and Dan obtained Bill Meyers' address from Pam and soon found themselves cruising down Johnstown Road, past a mixture of new housing and farmland. Just past a construction crew of busy men hammering and laying a concrete foundation, a barn on their left teetered dangerously to one side, and the sun shone through gaps in the decaying wooden planks. A rusted plow stood in the weed-filled field not far from the road.

"They ought to tear that thing down," Greg commented. "Is anyone farming there?"

"Probably retired or too old. He'll be selling out soon to the developers. Most of this'll be gone soon," Dan added.

"That guy's still going strong though," Greg said, pointing to a tractor pulling a plow through a five-acre field. The center of the field was dominated by two enormous oak trees whose trunks were so close together, they appeared at first as one tree.

Dan began to slow down and turned right just past the field onto Stonegate Drive, a long entrance road. They had arrived at the Stonegate Estates, one of the town's most lavish developments. The wide road was split in two by a concrete island that held a number of trees. There were a few mature myrtle trees, but most were Bradford pear ready to burst into flower. The buds gave the branches an appearance of being tipped by cotton balls. At the base of the trees, well-manicured flower beds completed a picture worthy of a magazine cover for fine home living. Stonegate Drive ended at a small pond with a fountain in its center spraying a shower of droplets into the air. They turned left onto Hill Drive, then made a right two streets down onto Cutbrook Road, past well-maintained lawns. Several people were outside, some cutting grass, others planting shrubs, and a few simply sitting on their porches with a glass of iced tea at hand.

"Wow, I bet they get a pretty penny for a house in this place," Greg mused aloud.

"You won't find anything here for less than a quarter-million, and most go for a lot more," Dan said confidently.

They followed Cutbrook several blocks to a cul-de-sac and swung around to stop at a two-story Colonial with Cape Cod windows and a tall loblolly pine on the front lawn.

"Eleven-oh-four—this is it," Dan said, and they got out of his Lexus.

As they walked to the front door, Greg caught a glimpse of a pond behind the house just as a trio of ducks came in for a noisy landing on the water. Behind a scalloped fence he could also see a large shed in the backyard and a small garden between the house and the shed. A garden tiller sat next to the shed, whose doors were open, and several tools were scattered about and leaning against it.

"Don't bother ringing the doorbell," Greg said.

"Why not?" Dan asked, but he stopped, his finger inches from the buzzer.

"Can I help you?" a female voice called from the backyard, and Dan followed Greg around the walkway to stand at the gate leading to the backyard.

A woman walked up to the fence. She was wearing a wide-brimmed white hat with a scarf tied around the rim, a pair of baggy khakis, and a long-sleeved pastel blouse. She held a small spade, which she switched from one hand to another as she pulled off a pair of garden gloves. A gust of wind nearly pulled her hat off, but she caught it just in time. The hat rose high enough for Greg to catch a glimpse of short red hair and milky, fair skin. Her high cheekbones and square jaw gave her a strong, confident appearance, and her emerald green eyes completed the sculpture. If she'd been a little taller than her five-foot-four-inch frame, she might have been a model instead of a teacher home after school, working in her garden.

"Sorry to bother you, Mrs. Meyers, but is your husband home?" Greg asked. At the same time he offered his identification for her inspection.

"Fish and Wildlife? This isn't about that duck, is it? I told Bill not to kill it, but they've been swimming in our pool, and they make such a mess. It's not like they're on the endangered species list," she said.

"No, ma'am, this isn't about a duck," Greg said, and he gestured toward Dan. "I'm Greg Parnell, and this is Special Agent Dan Brennan. Mr. Brennan is with the FBI."

"FBI?" she replied with an alarm that she quickly concealed. She spent several seconds examining Dan's credentials—time spent, Greg assumed, to gather her thoughts.

"Well, what can I do for you gentlemen?" she finally asked, and she opened the gate to allow them into the backyard. "I'm afraid I don't have much in the way of refreshments, but I could offer you some iced tea or a soda."

"We're fine, Mrs. Meyers," Dan replied. "We just need to speak with your husband. Is he home?"

"Call me Crystal," she offered. "Speak to him about . . . ?" she began, encouraging one of them to complete her sentence.

"Just routine," Greg said. "He may have information as a witness for an investigation we're conducting." It was true, if vague. He didn't want to reveal too much, lest Crystal alert her husband before they could question him. In this era of cell phones and instant communication, he had learned the value of withholding information. Her posture and tone suggested someone with an intense desire to know exactly what they wanted from her husband.

"I see," she said. "Well, I'm afraid he's not here at the moment. Can I give him a number where he can reach you?" she asked.

Before Greg could intervene, Dan handed her his card and said, "Both my work and home numbers are on the card. But it would be easier to talk to him in person. It would only take a few minutes. Does he have an office in town?"

"Actually, his office is in the house. We have four bedrooms, and he turned one of them into a home office. But you could probably find him at the Drummond site today.

"Drummond?" Dan asked.

"It's a new development being planned, just east of the Dismal Swamp," Greg explained. "Three hundred houses and a golf course, if I remember correctly." He was well aware of the development and aware that its proximity to the refuge was a hot topic of discussion among his co-workers.

"That's right," Crystal confirmed. "He spends most of his time there, when he's not in New York. He just got back from an overnight trip to Manhattan yesterday."

"New York? A little vacation?" Greg asked.

"I wish," Crystal said, chuckling. The action, combined with a smile, made her face glow, and for a moment Greg saw a beautiful woman behind the rigid control of a worried wife. "Actually, he was meeting with his bankers about the Drummond project. They're very interested in it. People just love this area, don't you think?"

"I know I do. Thanks for your help, Mrs., uh, Crystal," Greg said, correcting himself.

"Do we need directions?" Dan asked hesitantly.

"No, we're fine. I can get us there. Thanks again," Greg added, and he waved at Mrs. Meyers.

Dan followed him but turned when he heard Crystal ask, "What investigation was this about, did you say?"

To Greg's dismay, Dan replied, "The drowning of a woman in the Dismal Swamp a couple days ago."

When Dan slammed his car door shut and turned on the ignition, Greg stared at him. "Thanks a lot. Maybe we should have told her that her husband is a suspect."

"I said she drowned," Dan defended himself. "What do you want from me? Besides, he's just a witness at this point. We don't have any reason to suspect him yet, do we?" he asked.

"Just the same, there's no reason to advertise our interest," Greg complained. "Turn left when you get back to the entrance. We're headed out to Cedar Road."

Crystal Meyers watched the car drive away before she headed through the front door. She then picked up the cordless phone and dialed her husband's cell phone number. It rang four times before she began to mutter to herself.

"Come on, pick up, you fool. Pick up, pick up, pick UP!"

Bill Meyers heard the ring of the cellular phone, even as he continued to direct work from the edge of the Drummond development near Highway 17. The drainage was still taking too long, and he had devised a plan to increase the width of the ditches to speed the process. A large yellow earthmover straddled one of the freshly cut ditches, and he was looking at a map with his foreman and the operator. With some final instructions, the foreman walked away with the other man, and Bill glanced down at the cell phone display.

Crystal had called. He could call her later, or listen to the message she had undoubtedly left for him, when he had time. Right now, he wanted to think. He watched the machine's huge shovel swing into action as it gouged deep wounds in the ditch to widen it. The arm swung around, dumping a mixture of earth, sod, and water into the bed of a huge truck that would cart the debris away.

The effort would take several more days, a delay that Bill's bankers had not been happy to hear about. But even that was not at the forefront of his attention. Something else was bothering him. A few minutes later, the phone rang again. He looked at the display, and a small furrow appeared between his eyebrows. He again ignored the shrill sound. His attention was caught by something else. A car had pulled up next to his own vehicle.

Two men emerged from the silver Lexus. At first he

thought the man in the suit and tie might be his lawyer or accountant. But then he noticed the other man, and the uniform, and the weapon holstered by his side. The men spoke to the foreman, who began to point in his direction. Bill had barely enough time to turn his back to them. With quick stabbing movements, he pushed the buttons on his cell phone. He had decided that perhaps he would like to talk to his wife after all.

"He's over there," the foreman said, and he pointed to a tall figure in boots, blue jeans, and a red flannel shirt using a cell phone. Greg and Dan approached and halted about twenty feet away while their target murmured and grunted into the phone. Greg mouthed the word *wife* to Dan, who dismissed the suggestion.

"Mr. Meyers?" Dan began when Bill folded the phone and placed it back on his hip.

"Yes? Can I help you?" he said, extending a hand to shake.

"I'm Dan Brennan, FBI, and this is Greg Parnell, US Fish and Wildlife."

"Pleased to meet you," Bill said after the introduction and handshakes. "Work out of the refuge?" he asked, looking at Greg, who nodded. "I can assure you gentlemen that I have all the necessary permits and paperwork for the work you see being done. City officials should have told you that, but if you need to see them, that's not a problem. I'm always eager to cooperate to make your job easier."

"Actually, we're not here about the permits," Greg

said. "But I'm glad to hear you say that. We appreciate cooperation," he said, smiling.

"Well, what can I do for you?" Bill inquired.

"We're investigating a death in the swamp, a local woman found near the Jericho Ditch," Dan said. "We understand she was a friend of yours—Ashley Myrtle?"

"Yes, I heard about it when I returned from New York. Quite a shock that was, her drowning. I've known her husband for many years," he said. "The funeral's tomorrow, and he's asked me to be one of the pallbearers," he added.

"So, you've spoken with the councilman?" Greg asked.

"Oh, yes. I went over as soon as my wife told me about reading it in the paper. So senseless, drowning like that."

"We understand you had lunch with her on Tuesday, the day she died," Dan said.

"Um, yes, I did," Bill said. "Ironic, isn't it? I may have been the last person to see her. If I had known where she was going, I could have gone with her, and perhaps this wouldn't have happened."

"Where did you eat?" Dan asked.

"At the Courtyard Café, on Battlefield Boulevard. Do you know it?"

"Yes," Greg replied. Then he smiled and added, "The crab soup is to die for, don't you think?"

Bill smiled and looked at him. "What an odd choice of words," he said with a slight tremor in his voice.

"Oops, my apologies," Greg said.

"No problem," Bill replied.

"What did you talk about?" Greg asked.

"Oh, uh, nothing really. How's the family, how's work, same old, same old, you know."

"Tell her about the Drummond project?" Greg asked.

"Oh, yeah, but she's known about that for some time," Bill replied. His hands were now thrust into his jeans pockets, and he rocked slightly back and forth on his heels.

"Her work, what she was doing?" Greg asked.

"Yup, pretty much. She's really into saving the whales and everything. She loves to talk about that. Sometimes you couldn't shut her up," Bill said with a chuckle. Dan and Greg also nodded and chuckled.

"Did she talk about her report?" Dan asked.

"What report?" Bill asked, and he appeared genuinely perplexed.

"The report she was working on, for the Conservancy, on wetland conservation," Greg said.

Bill shook his head and stuck out his lower lip a bit. "Nope. Never mentioned it. Was it important?" Bill asked.

"Not really," Greg said nonchalantly. "I just assumed, since you were having lunch, that she wanted to meet you to talk about it. You did say that she talked about her work?" Greg asked, and Bill nodded a confirmation. "Anyway," Greg continued, "it seems that a lot of people were interested in this report. That's not why you met for lunch, to discuss it? After all, your development here depends on removing several dozen acres of wetlands."

"Actually, the lunch idea was pretty much a spontaneous thing. I was in the area, and I thought I'd call and see if she had any plans," Bill explained.

Dan opened a notebook and began to jot. "Who drove?" he asked.

"Um, I had my car," Bill said after a long moment's hesitation. The effect was not lost on Greg and Dan, and both men looked at Bill with questioning expressions.

"Sorry, I've been traveling so much, and it was a couple days ago. Had to think for a moment, busy schedule and all. Frankly, it's still a bit of a shock, the drowning."

"Sure, sure. I suppose you put in a lot of hours on this project," Greg said, and he looked around. "Wow. How many houses are you putting in?"

"We're planning three hundred homes and an eighteen-hole golf course," Bill said proudly. His chest puffed up, and he took his hands out of his pockets.

"Very impressive. These here, are these for a sewer line?" Greg asked, gesturing toward the gouges the earthmover was making.

"Actually, these are drainage ditches. They call them Tulloch ditches. They're basically to drain the land, to make it safe enough to build houses on," Bill explained.

"I see," Greg nodded. "Pretty lucky about that appeals case."

"What case?"

"The Federal Court of Appeals land use case. I was thinking of their decision, the one that said the Army

Corps of Engineers couldn't regulate building on wet-lands or prohibit drainage ditches. I suppose that would have made this project a little tougher to approve."

"Oh, yeah," Bill conceded. "Without it, I would have had to cancel this project. I've got everything I own in this baby."

"Pretty risky, isn't it?" Dan asked.

"This country was built on risk," Bill said with a smile. "But I didn't sink my stake in until after the decision came out. Most of it's being financed anyway. My stake's only twenty percent," he said.

"Anything else?" Greg asked Dan, who shook his head. "Well, I guess that's it. Thanks for your help."

"No problem," Bill said, and he began to walk them to their car.

"What did she think of all this?" Greg asked after they shook hands to leave.

"Who's that?" Bill asked.

"Ashley. What did she think of the development? I mean, I understand there was some local opposition. Did she, or the Conservancy, have an opinion on it?"

"Not that I know of. Like I said, we're old friends, Ashley and I. Besides, this little corner of the world isn't going to make any difference to the Bay," Bill assured him.

"I guess not. Well, thanks again."

Dan put the car into gear and drove off. At the edge of the road leading back to Route 17, he stopped the car and ran one hand slowly under his chin. "Anything seem strange about that conversation?" he asked.

"Well, he said that Ashley and he talked about her work. Then he claims that she never mentioned the report she was writing. It was her biggest project ever, according to the people at the Chesapeake Conservancy. Seems hard to believe she wouldn't talk about it with an old friend," Greg said.

"That's a good point. But what else?" Dan asked.

"Uh, he said the lunch was a spur-of-the-moment decision, but it was marked in her appointment book," Greg recalled.

"Yeah, but besides that," Dan pressed.

"Oh, you mean about how he mentioned the drowning, how she drowned. Said it a couple times, like he wanted there to be no doubt about it."

"Sort of, but that's not what I meant," Dan confessed.

"What did you mean?" Greg asked. "Don't keep me in suspense."

Dan turned to look at Greg, and he wore a very unsatisfied expression on his face. "Everyone we talked to so far has thought it strange that we wanted to interview them over a drowning. They got suspicious, like maybe there was more to it than a simple drowning . . . except for Bill. He never asked, he just accepted it, like it was normal that the FBI and US Fish and Wildlife would ask questions about it."

"Like maybe he was expecting us?" Greg asked. He raised a hand to his ear as though holding a phone to it. "Hello, honey, just wanted to let you know about the FBI asking for you. They're on their way over." Greg shrugged. "I told you not to tell his wife anything."

"Must feel good, huh?" Dan asked as he pulled into traffic and gunned the engine.

"What's that?" Greg asked, bracing himself on the dash as the car jerked forward.

"Being right, once in a great while," Dan quipped.

Chapter Twenty

The funeral was a private ceremony, at the request of Jonathan Myrtle, but several close advisors and friends made their appearance, including the governor, who stood next to Jonathan during the sermon at the graveside. The mayor attended as well, as expected but perhaps not as welcome.

"Ashley was a dear friend," the governor said at the conclusion of the ceremony, and he solemnly shook Jonathan's hand.

At that moment someone took a picture, and both men, so used to being in the spotlight, had to resist the instinct to smile on this solemn occasion. The mayor patiently waited for his turn to console his political rival and silently wondered if this opportunity to hold the governor's ear would help Jonathan in the upcoming election. Finally Mayor Greeley saw his chance and waded into the group.

"Governor."

"Mr. Mayor. Good of you to come. Such a tragedy. I understand that you have a couple of leads in this case?" he inquired. People moved away from the graveside as the three men convened an impromptu powwow.

"Yes, sir," the mayor said.

"No thanks to our own people," Jonathan added with a frown.

The governor nodded. He turned to the mayor and asked, "Ethan, I understand that the Great Bridge police are not leading the investigation?"

The mayor recognized the question and its implication that his own power had been usurped. "We're assisting the FBI in the case, but unfortunately, because the 'accident' took place on Federal property, we've had to defer to their authority," he explained.

"More like their intrusion," Jonathan added.

"Hmm. You know, if you need the assistance of the state police, I'm sure I can arrange it, make the necessary calls," the governor suggested.

"Thank you, Governor. I'll keep that in mind. For the moment, I think we can get by with what we have," Ethan said.

"Very well, then." The governor raised a hand and signaled to his driver, who went to retrieve the car. "Jonathan, I know how difficult this time has been for you. If you need anything, anything at all," the governor repeated, "call me."

He walked away, and Ethan remained by Jonathan's side. The two men began to walk toward the line of cars fighting for position at the cemetery exit.

"Jonathan, under the circumstances, no one will hold it against you if you decide to withdraw from the race. I certainly won't exploit this tragedy for my benefit," he said, stopping by his car. "But there'll be other races. Perhaps you should sit this one out."

"Thank you, Ethan. But I think Ashley would want me to continue. She was so much a part of this campaign. I wouldn't want to let her down, seeing as I've come this far," Jonathan said. Then he smiled and extended his hand.

"As you wish," Ethan said, and he shook his hand. He entered the backseat of the blue Ford Taurus and watched as his rival walked away.

"Well?" the driver said to Mayor Greeley from the front seat.

"He didn't take the bait," the mayor replied as he pulled on a pair of leather gloves. "He's dedicating this race to the memory of his wife, the little liar. That should bring in the votes, unfortunately."

"Then I suppose you'll be needing this," the driver said, and he handed back a manila envelope. The mayor opened it, removed a sheet of paper, read it briefly, nodded, and then placed it back in the envelope. He handed it back to the driver.

"Make sure the FBI agent in charge gets it. Dan Brennan, in the Norfolk office."

"Why not just give it to him yourself?"

"He knows that I'm running against Jonathan. It would be too obvious that I was trying to oust a competitor. This way, he'll come to me. After a few persistent questions, I'll reluctantly reveal that Jonathan did not, in fact, keep our appointment on the day his wife disappeared. The FBI can draw its own conclusions. But having a copy of Jonathan's appointment book for that day should help them a lot," the mayor said.

"Assuming he killed his wife," the driver said. "But what if he didn't?"

"It doesn't really matter, does it?" the mayor said. "The damage will be done, and the election will be over before the polls even open."

When Greg arrived, he was waved through by the security guard and escorted to a second-floor conference room. Dan was waiting outside the closed door. The two shook hands, then Dan briefly explained his game plan. Greg listened as he examined the folder he'd been handed.

"He came in voluntarily?" Greg asked, his eyes still on the folder.

"Yeah, but he brought his lawyer to act as a harness in case he gets too forthcoming. That's why I wanted you here, so we could play Good Cop, Bad Cop. He seems to like you, so you can be the Good Cop."

"Did you just say 'Good Cop, Bad Cop'?" Greg chuckled.

"I can see this was a mistake already." Dan frowned.

"No, no. I like it. Good strategy. It's just . . . I . . . okay, I'm ready" Greg said, stifling a chuckle.

Dan placed a hand on the doorknob.

"Wait."

Dan paused, a scowl forming on his face. Finally he hissed, "Are we going to do this or not?"

"Sorry. Okay, I'm ready," Greg said again.

Dan shook his head, then opened the door.

"Mr. Myrtle, thank you for coming in," Dan said as he pulled out a chair. He sat across from Jonathan Myrtle. Greg took a chair to Dan's right. He nodded to Jonathan, who nodded back, despite the glare he kept pasted on his face.

"I advised my client against this, but he insisted," a man seated next to Myrtle said.

"And you are?" Dan asked.

"Arthur Fullpincher."

"Is your client willing to answer a few questions?"

"It depends on what the questions are," Arthur said.

"Of course I am," Jonathan interrupted. "I've got nothing to hide."

"Jonathan, let's rethink this. You've just been through a traumatic experience. Perhaps we should do this another day," his lawyer urged.

"No," he said stubbornly. "Let's get this over with."

"Fine." Dan placed the manila folder on the desk, folded his arms, and leaned back in his chair. "Why don't you start by telling us where you were on the day your wife disappeared?"

"As I told you before, my secretary can provide you with my schedule. All you need to do is ask her."

"I'm asking you."

Jonathan sighed audibly. "I don't have my appointment book with me. If you'd informed me, I could have arranged to bring it."

"Would you like some coffee, Mr. Myrtle?" Greg suddenly asked. "I'm sorry, I should have offered before we began. How about you, Mr. Fullbladder? Coffee?"

"That's Fullpincher. And no, no coffee."

"Tea? Mr. Myrtle, sweet tea?" Greg continued.

"No, thank you."

"Well, then, where were we? You were about to tell us about your day. As I recall, you had several appointments," Dan said.

"My days are usually booked. As a city councilman, I have many constituents to serve," Jonathan explained.

"Naturally," Dan concurred. "A visit to the local VFW post, a meeting with the mayor, a speech for the planning committee of the Peanut Festival, a dedication at the zoo for a new exhibit. A busy day, wouldn't you say, Mr. Myrtle?" Dan asked.

Jonathan Myrtle looked at Dan with confusion and, for a moment, what looked like fear, but the appearance turned almost immediately to the same glare he'd been wearing since Greg and Dan entered the room. "If you know my schedule, why are you bothering me with it again?" he asked.

"How'd the dedication go?"

"What?"

"The dedication. At the zoo. They're opening a new reptile house, aren't they?"

"I can't wait to see that," Greg added. "A lot of their specimens are going to come from right here, in the Dismal Swamp. Kinda makes you proud, doesn't it, Mr. Myrtle?"

"So, how'd it go?" Dan asked again.

"What does that have to do with anything?" Jonathan protested.

"How about the meeting with the mayor? What was that about?"

"I don't think my political consultations are any of your business," Jonathan said, waving a hand at Dan in dismissal.

"He may be right, you know," Greg said, turning to Dan. "Maybe he was discussing some city business, totally unrelated to his wife's disappearance." He turned to Jonathan. "Is that it? City business with the mayor? If it was, just tell us. I understand that sort of thing," he said warmly.

"Not exactly," Jonathan said slowly, looking at Greg as if trying to read the younger man's intentions.

"What he means by 'not exactly' is that he didn't meet with the mayor," Dan said. He leaned forward and tapped on the folder. "Did you, Mr. Myrtle?"

"I'll have to check my notes and get back to you."

"Oh, come on! Your notes? Can't you remember a meeting from just a few days ago?" Dan asked.

"I'm a very busy man."

"I can buy that," Greg said with a nod.

"Where is this going?" Arthur interjected.

"The fact is," Dan said, and he began to tap on the folder with one finger, "you didn't meet with the mayor, you were a no-show at the VFW, the Peanut Festival committee had to reschedule your speech, and you missed the dedication at the zoo."

"I don't know where you're getting your information, but I think you've been misinformed," Jonathan said.

"I don't think so," Dan replied. He opened the folder and turned it around so Jonathan could read it.

"According to your own notes, you cancelled every appointment you had for that day. Didn't you?" Dan asked.

"What? Why, that's a page from my appointment book!" Jonathan protested.

"Jonathan, don't say another word," Arthur warned. "That information is confidential, and you've got no warrant," he said to Dan.

"Really? Are you sure it's yours? Maybe it's a forgery," Greg suggested.

"Of course I'm sure. I should know my own writing!" Jonathan howled.

"Thank you for confirming that," Dan said.

"What? Oh, that's your game, is it?" Jonathan said. He looked at Dan, then at Greg, and pointed a finger at him. "I would have expected something like this from the FBI, but coming from you, Mr. Parnell—I'm surprised you would try to trick me."

"I was just trying to be helpful," Greg said with a shrug.

"You still haven't answered my question. Where did you get that?" Arthur demanded.

"It came by messenger service this morning from an anonymous source," Dan said.

"A likely story," Jonathan said.

"I can show your lawyer the messenger's receipt if you like."

"This meeting is over. Let's go, Jonathan," Arthur urged, and he stood. He grabbed Jonathan by the arm, and the man rose to his feet. "I suppose you've already talked to Ethan Greeley," Jonathan said. "Don't you realize he probably sent that to you to embarrass me?"

"The thought did cross our minds," Greg admitted.

"But the mayor was reluctant to talk to us at first. He finally admitted that the meeting had been cancelled at your request. That's all he would tell us," Dan said.

"He doesn't seem the type to play tricks," Greg said.

"Besides, you can clear all this up very easily," Dan said.

"How's that?" Jonathan asked, pausing at the conference room door.

"Not another word," Arthur said.

"Just tell us where you were," Greg urged. "I'm sure you had a very good reason for cancelling those appointments."

"Very well," Jonathan growled.

"You don't have to answer that," Arthur said.

"I was in Richmond, attending a parole hearing for a

former staff member of mine," Jonathan said, ignoring the tug at his arm from his lawyer.

"A parole hearing?" Dan said incredulously.

"Yes. I spent most of the day preparing and then went to Richmond to plead his case. The man made a mistake, but he's paid for it. Tax evasion, if you must know. And unlike some people, we here in the South don't abandon our friends in their time of need. Four o'clock. You can check with the commonwealth's parole board, if you like. They'll confirm it," Jonathan said.

"We will," Dan replied.

"Satisfied? C'mon, Jonathan," Arthur urged.

"With pleasure." He slammed the door behind him.

Dan glanced at Greg.

"If his excuse pans out, he could be in the clear," Greg said, and he shrugged.

"Four o'clock. I don't think that's good enough," Dan suggested. "Ashley left the Conservancy at eleven-thirty. An hour lunch with Bill Meyers, and then she vanished. That still gave Jonathan two hours to kill his wife and move the body."

"How do you figure?" Greg asked.

"It only takes ninety minutes to drive to Richmond," Dan said.

Chapter Twenty-one

Greg and Dan agreed to split up some of their tasks for the next day and to meet the day after that. Dan wanted to search the computers at the Conservancy, specifically Ashley's and Earl's, and he needed to secure permission from the board of directors. Lacking that, he felt that he had enough information for a search warrant, but he wanted to try the soft route first. He didn't think the board would have any objections once he outlined his suspicions about Ashley's death, and he was sure that the board would want to obtain a copy of the elusive wetlands report Ashley had written.

Greg intended to get a copy of Ashley's divorce filing. Once Greg and Dan met again, they wanted to reinterview Jonathan Myrtle and then sit down to compare notes. It seemed like a simple plan, but something so simple in a small town like Great Bridge often became complex, where many interpersonal relationships were involved.

"What do you mean, you have no record of the divorce filing?" Greg asked, perplexed. He had just finished reviewing a list of divorce petitions given to him in the office of the Family Court. The Myrtle name appeared nowhere on it. Now Greg found himself standing across from a clerk, who, an hour before, had been so cooperative on the phone.

"I'm sorry, Mr. Parnell, I must have been mistaken," she said with an air of confusion.

"Wait a minute. Back up," Greg said, raising his hands in front of him. "When I called and asked about the Myrtle divorce filing, you told me that it was dropped off this past Monday. Now you say it isn't here?"

"No, I'm saying that I must have misunderstood you," she said with a chilly tone. "It happens sometimes."

"Confusion about the name? I don't think so," Greg asserted. "In fact, when I mentioned the name Myrtle, you asked me if I was referring to Ashley and Jonathan. I didn't even give you first names, but you knew who I was talking about."

"Well, I don't remember saying that. All the records that have been registered with the court are right there. I don't know what else to tell you." Her arms were folded across her chest, and her face appeared stoic and hard.

It was becoming clear to Greg that he wasn't going to resolve this with an underling. "All right. If that's the way you want it. I'd like to talk to the your supervisor," Greg stated, and he folded his own arms.

The woman didn't speak but simply turned and began to walk to a far corner of the long, open room, where a tall, balding man sat in a swivel chair at a gray metal desk. He had been observing the exchange between Greg and the clerks and rose before she even reached his desk. He nodded as she spoke to him in a low voice. Greg could not make out the words, but he appeared to placate her, because she returned to her own desk with a final defiant glare at Greg.

Greg placed a hand to his forehead and swore under his breath. Perhaps small-town life wasn't going to be as dull as he'd feared, but it was turning out to be frustrating.

"Mr. Parnell, I'm Stanley Walters. Why don't we sit down? Perhaps I can sort this out for you," he said. He extended a hand, which Greg reluctantly shook. Stanley opened a gate that allowed Greg into the office area, and the two men walked back to the corner. Greg took a seat next to the desk.

"Do you know I'm investigating Ashley Myrtle's death, Mr. Walters? This isn't a personal request. If I need to secure a warrant to get the records, I will do so," Greg began, ready to fight.

Stanley held up a hand. "That won't be necessary. I guess I should have handled this when you called. Ashley's lawyer did drop off a petition for divorce on Monday. But we were a little backed up, so we didn't file it right away. That's why it's not in the records. Mrs. Plimpsel, my clerk, was simply being discreet. And since Ashley's now dead, well, there didn't seem to be any reason to record it."

"I see," Greg said. "Thanks for your honesty. But it's not up to you to make that decision about the filing. It really has to become part of the official record," Greg insisted. Stanley remained silent, much to Greg's surprise. After a moment he said, "Well, can I see it?"

"I don't have it anymore," Stanley replied.

"What?" Greg exclaimed, a little louder than he'd intended. A couple of people at their desks looked up. "Where is it?" he asked in a lowered voice.

"Jonathan Myrtle picked it up this morning," Stanley announced.

"After you called him on Monday, no doubt," Greg said. It was a statement rather than a question.

"That's not true," Stanley insisted with a pointed finger.

"So you never spoke to him?" Greg asked. "On the record, Mr. Walters," he emphasized, and he removed a notebook and pen from his pocket.

Stanley Walters leaned back in his chair. "Okay, I did speak with him," he confessed. "But only after it was reported that Ashley had been found dead. I simply wanted to express my condolences. That's when he asked me about the petition. He'd been served the day before."

"He asked you for it?" Greg queried. Stanley nodded affirmatively. "And you didn't think that suspicious?" Greg pressed.

"The article in the paper said that she drowned," Stanley insisted. Then his face changed, and a look of alarm replaced his defensive stance. "She did drown, didn't she?"

"The official cause of death hasn't been released, but it looks that way," Greg said, without adding that it didn't look that way to him. "Still, you had no right to return that document. I wonder what her lawyer will say about it," Greg speculated.

"Hasn't that family suffered enough?" Stanley said, and he made a sound as though he were tsk-tsking a young child for misbehavior. "She's being buried as we speak."

At that moment, a new thought occurred to Greg. "How long have you known Jonathan Myrtle, personally, Mr. Walters?" Greg asked softly.

"I've know Jonathan for almost twenty years," he said, "And I can tell you this, you'll never meet a nicer man, especially when it comes to remembering the little people. He's done a lot for this town, and he still remembers the people he met on the way up. Not like some politicians I could name."

"He got you this job, didn't he?" Greg asked.

"I was elected to this position, Mr. Parnell," he said stiffly, using Greg's surname. "But Jonathan did endorse me. That's not why I'm defending him, though. He's earned my respect by his actions."

Greg closed his notebook and put it back into his pocket. It seemed pointless to blame a county clerk for what had happened. At any rate, he would have to get the petition from Jonathan, most likely with a warrant. He stood to leave, and Stanley stood also.

"Thanks, anyway, for being forthright," Greg said as

he shook the man's hand. "I have to admire your loyalty as well."

"We have nothing to hide. It's just that these were rather unusual circumstances, and I saw no need to rub salt in the man's wounds," Stanley said. "As for loyalty, that's something we don't see much of in the world these days. I think we need a little more of it."

Greg left the Great Bridge municipal building with a very unsatisfied sense of accomplishment, but he wasn't sure there was anything he could do about it. On the way back to headquarters, he suddenly thought that perhaps some breakfast would make him feel better. He'd only had some leftover coffee at the house, then rushed out the door. With the urge for caffeine on his mind, he continued down Battlefield Boulevard after turning off of Cedar Road, and he pulled into The Grill, hoping to find space at the counter. The possibility that Amanda would be working also entered his mind as he parked the car.

He entered to find her sister working the tables, her parents behind the counter, but no sign of Amanda. He took a seat at the end of the counter.

"Hi, Greg," Angie greeted him from behind the counter. She pulled a pencil from behind one ear and held it suspended above a notepad. "The usual?"

Greg nodded and looked around as Julie filled a cup of coffee for him. He nodded and smiled as she smiled. She moved out from behind the counter to refill some cups at the tables, and as she passed him, she leaned over and whispered, "Amanda's in class this morning, but she said to tell you hello."

Greg smiled to himself. He was glad to discover that she was thinking of him, but he didn't say so to Julie. He wanted to reserve that pleasure for himself, when he saw Amanda in person. He sipped his coffee after fortifying it with cream and sugar. Then he turned and nodded at the other patrons at the counter. He recognized a couple of the older men with baseball caps, one a crabber and the other a peanut farmer. They were debating the virtues of installing a new, wider toll road on Route 168 to give the tourists quicker access to the Outer Banks.

Greg decided to stay out of the conversation and concentrate on the murder. As unpleasant as it seemed, there were at least three possible suspects.

The husband was the natural choice for anyone who knew the least bit about criminal statistics, and despite Greg's initial sympathy for the man, he could not be ruled out. His alibi for the day of Ashley's disappearance was weak. From what little he knew about the man, it was difficult to draw any conclusions, but Jonathan apparently had a lot of power in local politics, since he could make an official court document disappear.

A twenty-five-year marriage on the rocks, he thought, a local politician in a conservative community, and maybe, most important, the feelings of betrayal that accompany any divorce. It was more than enough to create a motive for murder. Angie slid his plate in front of him on the counter, and Greg broke his reflection long enough to acknowledge her and pick up a fork.

Earl Thompson had several strikes against him also, Greg decided. He was short-tempered, which was obvious, and had a strong attachment, perhaps even an obsession, with Ashley. But was that a motive for murder? Earl didn't seem the type to be a stalker. Still, he couldn't account for his whereabouts at the time of Ashley's disappearance, and it seemed inconceivable that no one had seen him if he were at the Conservancy's office as he claimed. He said that he lent Ashley his truck, but that was impossible . . . unless the murderer had gone with her and returned alone.

It was possible, Greg thought, that Earl had offered to take her, and she had accepted. He could have slipped out the back door and met Ashley when she emerged out front. But why would Ashley fail to mention this to anyone? Was it possible that Earl's feelings hadn't been one-sided?

Greg realized suddenly that this didn't make sense. Ashley had lunch that day with Bill Meyers. Thus, she couldn't have left the Conservancy with Earl, unless he had dropped her off and picked her up after her lunch meeting. He made a note to check that out.

He was flipping through his notebook when he came upon a note he had made about receiving Brad's report on a case of vandalism. Brad had interviewed a bird-watcher who had seen an act of vandalism in the refuge at the Washington Ditch gate. The vandal had driven a white truck, and Earl had a white truck, Greg recalled. Brad had mentioned to Greg yesterday that the lock appeared damaged but not broken, as though someone had tried to file through it. As a field researcher, Earl would undoubtedly have a lot of useful equipment in his truck, including, perhaps, a set of tools and maybe even a metal file. He would need to mention it to Dan. It might be enough for a search warrant, although he personally doubted it.

The last suspect, Bill Meyers, seemed the least likely candidate for murder, although he was apparently the last person to see Ashley alive. He was calm during their interview, but Greg felt sure he had been warned of their arrival. Still, the man did not appear to have a clear motive yet. The Conservancy's report on wetland preservation might lead to severe restrictions on housing development in the area, including the Drummond Estates. But since the report had not turned up, he couldn't be sure what its impact might be. Unless Bill had murdered Ashley and taken the report.

It hardly seemed possible that Ashley would carry around the only copy of the report on her. He'd know more once Dan had examined Ashley's computer. Another small but significant item stuck in Greg's mind. Although he hadn't mentioned it to Dan, Greg noticed that the boots that Bill Meyers had worn on the day they interviewed him were made by Timberland. His foot size seemed rather large as well. But again, it would take a warrant to determine if those boots matched the print at the murder scene, and a warrant would never be granted on a few suspicions.

"Anything wrong?" a voice asked.

His fork still in his hand at the edge of the plate, Greg looked up to find Angie smiling at him.

"I can get you something else," she offered.

"No, I'm fine," Greg reassured her. "Just lost in thought, that's all." He plunged his fork into the hash browns and took a mouthful.

She leaned in to whisper, "Is it that Ashley woman the body found in the swamp?"

Greg nodded. "We're still investigating it," he said, and he grabbed a bite of eggs. "Food's fine," he added.

"Oh, good," she said. Then, returning to the Myrtle case, she added, "Amanda was talking about it all day yesterday. It's such a shame. Is it true what the paper said, that she may have been killed instead of drowning?" Her voice seemed to carry a trace of excitement, and Greg reflected on the morose interest people often had in murder cases. He knew it was true, because he sometimes felt it himself.

"Oh, I really can't comment on it," Greg admitted, eager to switch the subject.

"I understand," she whispered, and she patted his hand. "Good luck. You be careful, now," she said, and she went off to clear some plates.

His attention back on his plate, Greg eagerly finished the rest of his food. He was mopping up the last of his yolk with a piece of toast when he felt a tug at his sleeve. He looked to his left to be greeted with the smile of Todd, the old crab fisherman.

"Arnie just bought my breakfast. Maybe he'll buy

yours too," Todd said with a smile. He turned to the other man, a peanut farmer. "Hey, Arnie, wanna buy this young man some breakfast? Are you a policeman?" he asked, returning his attention to Greg.

"What happened, you win the lottery?" Greg asked Arnie.

"Sure did. Sold my farm to a land developer three months ago. Just got the check last week," he said, and he pulled out a photocopy of a cashier's check to show Greg. "Five-hundred seventy-thousand free and clear, look at that. Lot 015-26. That's over by the Dismal Swamp. Ain't that your neck of the woods, Ranger Rick?"

Greg looked at the paper Arnie held under his nose. "Very nice. Congratulations," he said politely. It was time to go, Greg thought, before he was corralled into a long, boring speech. He dumped seven dollars and some change onto the counter and waved to Angie.

"Thanks for coming," Stan, her husband as well as the cook, said as Greg moved to the door.

Arnie was still talking as Greg exited. "Yes, sir, Lot 015-26, my lucky lotto number," the voice repeated.

When Greg walked into the refuge headquarters, he asked for Brad, but Cindy confirmed that he was in the field with some volunteers, clearing away a fallen tree on Portsmouth Ditch. "Ask him to talk to me when he's back," Greg said. He wanted to go over the vandalism report, perhaps see if the bird-watcher had a better description.

"Oh, the sheriff's department called—Deputy Green. He said that someone called to report seeing a light on in the Chesapeake Conservancy offices. Tuesday night around midnight. Local police drove by ten minutes later, but the place was secure, so they let it go."

"I'll call them tomorrow and see if someone was working late," Greg said, referring to the Chesapeake Conservancy.

"The police already did. Carol, the office manager, said no one should have been there. They're going to do an inventory to see if anything is missing after Dan finishes checking the computers. He even has FBI forensics dusting for prints. But there was no forced entry, and Deputy Green checked with the coroner. Ashley's keys were not found on her body. Interesting, no?" Cindy asked.

"Very. Are you thinking what I'm thinking?"

"I have some more interesting news," Cindy said. She handed him a typed statement on letterhead from the Great Bridge sheriff's department. "Deputy Green just faxed it over. I thought you'd want to see it right away," she said.

Greg scanned the single-page document and tapped it with a finger. "Now, this could really be something," he remarked, his voice rising. "I'll be in Floyd's office." He rushed into the room and picked up the phone to call Dan. He got the agent's voice mail and left him a message about the fax and the police report from Tuesday night. He picked up the fax again and smiled. *Maybe this*, he thought, *would give them enough for a warrant.*

Chapter Twenty-two

"So, who do you think did it?" Amanda asked in a low voice. She leaned close to Greg as she filled his coffee cup. Greg could smell her freshly washed hair and feel the warmth of her breath on his cheek. He motioned to her, and she turned her ear to his mouth.

"Well, in cases like this, it's almost always the husband. But my money's on either one of her co-workers or a family friend," he said.

Amanda turned back to look at him with shock in her eyes. "You don't say! A boyfriend?" she asked.

"Well, we're not sure, but it's possible."

"A secret love affair. Oh, my!" she said, patting her heart. "Of course, that would also give the husband a perfect motive, don't you think?" she asked.

Greg nodded, then motioned for her to come closer. When she complied, he added, "You can't say anything to anyone, not even family. I shouldn't even be telling you this."

"You can trust me," Amanda reassured him. "I took Intro to Criminal Justice, and we had a chapter on this same issue, ethics and all that stuff." She crossed her chest and gave him the scout's honor hand pledge. "On my honor," she added.

Greg smiled and motioned her close again. "Would you like to go to dinner one night next week?"

She looked at him and smiled broadly. "Yes, I would," she whispered before she left to take an order.

Greg felt a sudden flutter and tried to hide it. He nodded at everyone he saw as he sipped his coffee while waiting for his food. He would have to eat in a hurry. He was meeting Dan at the FBI building in Norfolk in just over an hour to go over what he had found. Dan might have a preliminary report on the forensics, and Greg was particularly eager to see what the computers held. He spread out the fax he had received and flipped through his notebook, going over all the evidence, the interviews, and his personal recollections. He looked up when he heard the voice of Arnie, the now retired peanut farmer, who joined his friend Todd two stools away at the counter.

"Angie, it's the Lotto man. He's gonna buy me breakfast again, ain't ya, Arnie?" Todd said.

"Hey, Lotto man," Angie said, adopting the nickname. She took his order, and Arnie began to retell his tale of sudden wealth to another man at the counter who apparently had not yet heard the story. Greg listened in with one ear as he reviewed his notes.

"Sold my peanut farm to a land developer. Look at that, a copy of my check. Five-hundred seventy-thousand dollars. Got my check last week. Lot 015-26, that's my lucky number. Just call me the Lotto man. Hey, what's the hurry, young fella?" Arnie asked.

He was staring at Greg, who was gulping the last of his coffee as he stood by his stool. He fished a ten-dollar bill out of his wallet and dropped it onto the counter just as Angie set down his plate.

"Sorry, I can't stay," he said apologetically. "May I borrow this?" he asked the startled peanut farmer, and he reached for the photocopy of the check.

"That's okay, take your money, Greg," Angie said, but Greg had already opened the door. He caught Amanda's eye and smiled at her before he jogged to his car. He halted when he heard a woman's voice call his name. It was Amanda.

"Please be careful," she called out to him. He smiled and blew her a kiss, which caused the worried look on her face to change to a smile. As he pulled the car out of the parking lot, she returned the gesture.

He would have felt great if he weren't mentally reprimanding himself for missing such a vital clue, which had literally hovered under his nose. It might not be the crucial piece of the puzzle, but Greg was convinced of one thing, at least. Bill Meyers must have lied when he said that Ashley did not discuss her report at their lunch. If only they had the report, it could clear up a lot of questions. He would be at Dan's office earlier than he had expected, but with any luck, Dan would be an early riser.

His luck held out. "He just got in," the receptionist said. "If you take the elevator to the seventh floor, I'll let him know you're on your way up."

Greg thanked her and nodded as he showed his badge to the guard, who waved him through the metal detector. After a short ride in a bumpy elevator, he walked down the fake-wood–paneled hall to a small office on his left. Dan waved to him and gathered a pile of folders off his desk. He stepped into the hall.

"My office is a little small. Let's use the conference room," he said, and he led Greg back the way he had come to a large room with a long table and ten chairs. A blackboard hung on the wall to their right, still dusty with chalk scribblings, which Dan erased. They were joined a moment later by a man with silver hair in his late fifties, Greg guessed. The man had an unlit pipe in his mouth and the scent of vanilla-flavored tobacco on his clothing.

"Ah, here he is. Greg, meet my boss, Brian Baxter. Brian, this is Greg Parnell with the US Fish and Wildlife Service," Dan said as he introduced the two.

"Well, well. It's a pleasure to meet you, Mr. Parnell," Brian said, and he shook his hand warmly. "My agent here says that you've practically got this case solved already. Thinks you're a real whiz."

"Really?" Greg said. "I'm pleased to hear that. A little surprised, as well, but pleased nonetheless." He stole a glance at Dan as they took seats.

"Remember, he's FBI—used to interrogating criminal suspects, so he's trained to lie well," Dan said jokingly.

"It's your show," Brian remarked.

Dan passed a folder to each of the men and opened the last, which he kept.

"Okay, I wanted to spend this morning just reviewing what we have so far, and give you our preliminary findings on the search of the Conservancy offices. Also, Greg left me a message saying he had some new evidence. A fax?"

"Got it here," Greg said, and he pulled out his fax, as well as the copy of the cashier's check he had practically stolen from Arnie at The Grill only minutes before. "I guess I should have made copies," he said belatedly.

"I'll do that," Brian offered. "How about a profile of each of the suspects? We can list them on the board."

"Sounds good," Dan said, and he wrote three names across the top of the blackboard while Brian went to copy the fax Greg had received. "This is where the fun begins," Dan cracked.

For the next two hours Dan and Greg reviewed the interviews they had jointly conducted, as Brian listened. They outlined possible motives of the three main suspects. Greg told of his encounter at the Family Clerk's office, and how Jonathan Myrtle had managed to keep the divorce petition a secret. Brian speculated that this action by itself was enough for a search warrant, since the petition was part of the public record as soon as it was delivered to the clerk's office. The FBI had found Ashley's report, which had been deleted from her computer but had been recovered with special software.

A copy had also been found on Earl's computer, but it was a different version. Dan went over the differences, which mainly consisted of a harsher tone in Earl's version, with a final recommendation far more restrictive than the one Ashley proposed. Dan thought that Earl might have pressured Ashley to adopt a more militant position, and when she resisted, he might have killed her and deleted her copy of the report, planning to replace it with his own. She did, however, recommend that a newly begun development be halted just east of the Dismal Swamp. Her version of the report did not name the development but did give a lot number, 015-26.

"That was the same number on Ashley's appointment book, just below her lunch date with Bill Meyers," Greg reminded Dan. "It wasn't a lock combination. It was the lot number for Bill's development at Drummond Estates. I bet she told him all about it at lunch. He paid over a half million dollars for that property, according to this check. He stood to lose a bundle when her report came out. That's an awfully big motive."

Dan searched his notes and finally found his own reference to Ashley's appointment book. "Looks like egg on my face. Didn't even see that. And I can't believe you got a copy of the seller's check already," he confessed. "How in the world did you manage that?"

"I just know the right people," Greg said simply.

Brian took the pipe from his mouth. "Nice work, son," he said to Greg, who blushed.

"Told you," Dan said to his boss. Then, addressing Greg, he added, "I'll confirm it at the municipal building on Monday." Dan picked up another sheet of paper. Then, of course, there is the fax you got from the Great Bridge sheriff's department. This statement from Mary Bailey really strengthens my argument for suspecting Earl, don't you think?"

"True enough," Greg confessed.

"This woman, she's a fund-raiser for the organization?" Brian asked.

"Yes. She wasn't there the day we interviewed Earl. But according to her statement, she overheard Ashley and Earl arguing a week ago last Friday, three days before she disappeared in the swamp. She states that Ashley accused Earl of snooping through her desk and told him that he had to stop obsessing over her," Greg paraphrased.

"My divorce has nothing to do with you, Earl. There can never be anything between us. If I gave you the wrong impression, I apologize. Now please leave my office," Brian read from the faxed statement, quoting Mary's recollection of the event. He removed his glasses and tossed the fax onto the desk. "Better talk to her and confirm it. Talk to Earl again. In fact," he added, "you probably need to talk to all three suspects again at some point. In the meantime, who's your favorite horse?" Brian asked, and he looked at the two of them.

"My money's on Earl, to win," Dan said confidently.

Brian nodded and turned to Greg.

"I like Earl too, but I think I like Bill Meyers more.

He had more to lose," Greg confessed. "How about you, sir?" Greg asked.

Brian leaned back in his chair and surveyed the blackboard, which was now covered in writing. "Gentlemen, I'm playing the odds. In the end, it usually comes back to the husband."

"So, who gets the search warrant?" Dan asked.

"Looks like they all had sufficient motive," Greg said.

"Let's get three warrants," Brian decided, "and see if we can shake an apple out of the tree."

Chapter Twenty-three

"What is the meaning of this?" Jonathan Myrtle roared from the doorway of his private office in the Great Bridge municipal building. A search warrant was handed to him, and he grabbed it and ripped it into several pieces. As he dropped it to the floor of the outer office, he ground his heel into the shreds of paper.

"Sorry, sir, you'll have to wait outside," said a man who wore a dark jacket emblazoned with the letters *FBI* on the back. Two other men dressed the same were going through drawers while another hooked up the computer to a portable CD burner with a USB cable.

"I'm sorry, Councilman, I tried to stop them," said a short, heavyset woman wearing a flowery-print blouse and black pants. "Oh, be careful with that vase. It's leaded crystal," she called to one of the men. "Oh, dear!"

"It's all right, Rose. It's not your fault. It's these carpetbaggers! They have no respect for decent people," he announced with a glaring scowl at the men moving around them.

"Please, sir. You must vacate this office until the search is complete," the man repeated.

Jonathan stood his ground until he saw Greg outside the office in the hallway, keeping back a crowd of city workers and other onlookers. Jonathan rushed past the men and charged at Greg.

"I would have expected this from the FBI, but not from you!" he said accusingly. "All your sympathetic words when you came to my house . . . my wife isn't even cold in her grave!"

"Mr. Myrtle, I am sorry for this intrusion," Greg said slowly. Jonathan dismissed his apology with a wave of his hand and turned his back on Greg, choosing to gaze at a hallway painting of Virginia's Washington College and its campus. "But a man of your experience surely must admit that the husband is always a logical suspect in cases like this one."

"And a man of your intelligence," Jonathan said over his shoulder, "surely must admit that the husband is not necessarily the only suspect." He kept his back to Greg and thrust his hands into his pant pocket.

"Quite true," Greg concurred. "Sometimes he is not even the prime suspect," he said in a lowered voice, and he walked to stand beside Jonathan. Greg gazed up at the painting but said nothing more.

Finally Jonathan could not tolerate the silence and

spoke, as Greg suspected he might. But this time his voice was inquiring instead of accusing.

"You have other suspects?" he asked Greg without removing his gaze from the painting.

"Naturally," Greg said, and nothing more.

After a few moments Jonathan spoke again. "And they are?" he asked.

"Under the circumstances," Greg explained, "I'm sure you understand why I can't be more specific, sir. You'd hardly trust me if I were, and I have too much respect for you."

Both men stared at the painting for a few more moments. Jonathan turned to see Rose, his secretary, standing patiently just out of hearing range, an anxious look on her face. Jonathan turned to go but paused and looked at the taller man. "You, sir, are a gentleman, much as I hate to say so. Not many people tell me no and still trouble themselves to stroke my ego at the same time." Greg moved as if to speak, but Jonathan held up a hand, gave a slight, sad smile, and rejoined his secretary and staff.

Greg checked back with the agents in the office. Ashley's report had not shown up, but much of the councilman's computer data would still need to be analyzed. Satisfied that he was not needed at the moment, he walked down the hallway out of the range of spectators to call Dan.

"Brennan here," a voice answered after one ring.

"How's your babysitting gig going?" Greg asked.

"The baby is very unhappy. Looks ready to throw a

temper tantrum. I had to threaten to spank him when we showed up, but he got the message. How about you?"

"Mr. Myrtle was upset, but I managed to sweet-talk him," Greg said. "It's all in the delivery."

"Ah, I wouldn't have bothered, but you do what you want. Some people only respond to a show of force, like our friend Earl."

"You catch more flies with honey than you do with vinegar," Greg countered.

"Did your mother teach you to be such a gentleman?" Dan joked.

"I thought you were my mother," Greg replied.

"Don't try and sweet-talk *me,* Jeremiah Johnson."

"When do we serve the last warrant?" Greg asked.

"Probably not until tomorrow, maybe the day after. I've got more agents at Myrtle's residence, and he owns three other buildings that we have to search. We just don't have the manpower, buddy. Meyers will have to wait," Dan concluded.

"Think he suspects?" Greg asked.

"Let's hope not. I don't think we gave him any reason to believe we were suspicious of him."

"His wife certainly was. Maybe we should talk to her as well," Greg speculated.

"That's an idea. We could double-team them. Why don't we meet at my office, say around five, talk about it," Dan said.

"Sounds good," Greg replied before he hung up.

He checked his watch. It was still early, only a little after ten. Dan would be running the rest of the day, and

Greg thought that it was the perfect opportunity to check back in at the refuge headquarters and get some work done. Floyd was still in Florida and by now expected an update on their progress. Greg had called him daily, but, with little to report, the calls had been short. Now that the warrants had been issued, there was a lot to discuss, and Floyd would undoubtedly have questions.

Greg left the municipal building and took his time getting back to the refuge for a change. He wondered which way would the evidence point. They would all know very soon.

Greg called his boss at two and spent nearly an hour debriefing Floyd. His manager had been edgy about being away for a week, but by the end of Greg's update, Floyd felt comfortable enough to postpone his return for a couple more days. It would give him time to make funeral arrangements.

"I'll let everyone here know. Sorry again about your mom," Greg said sincerely.

"She went peacefully. I'm glad all the kids were here," Floyd said. He sounded very tired. "Well, keep up the good work. I gotta go."

"See you soon," Greg said. He looked at his watch. It was almost three o'clock. He calculated he still had ninety minutes to fill. He was wrong. The phone rang, but he ignored it, hoping Cindy would pick up. After six rings he picked it up, but not without a sense of irritation. Where had Cindy gone?

"Dismal Swamp Refuge," he announced.

"Get yourself up here right away." It was Dan. "I've been trying to reach you for almost an hour."

"You got something?" Greg asked. A lump formed in his throat.

"You bet. Oh, and bring that combination lock, the one from the Washington Ditch gate."

"The lock? What do you need that for?"

"Just bring it! We need to match it to some evidence we found."

"Okay, okay," Greg conceded. "I'm on my way. Who was it?" he asked.

"You'd like to know, wouldn't you?" Dan said, and he chuckled.

"Of course!" Greg replied.

"Then hurry up," Dan replied, and he hung up. It was not the answer Greg had expected.

"Cindy! I need another lock for the Washington Ditch gate!" Greg yelled into the hallway. Cindy quickly appeared, and they both searched through the offices, while Greg explained that he would be taking the current lock to the FBI for analysis. All they could turn up was an old lock with a single key that had to be wiggled violently to open the cylinder.

"It'll have to do," Greg said. He looked at Cindy and added, "By the way, Floyd's mother died in her sleep last night."

Cindy held her hands to her face. "I'm sorry to hear that."

Greg hesitated. "Maybe I should tell the others."

She shook her head and waved him out the door. "I'll handle it," she said. "Go get that murderer."

Greg expected to find Dan on the seventh floor, but the agent was waiting for him in the lobby of the Federal building. As soon as Greg passed through the metal detector, Dan hit the elevator button.

"What took you so long?" Dan asked, but he was all smiles. "Got the lock? We're going to the fourth floor."

Greg handed it to him. "What's on four?"

"A microscope and a forensic expert," Dan replied. "We need some filings from the lock to see if they match shavings we recovered from a toolbox."

"Whose?" Greg asked eagerly.

"Hang on, hang on. Have to confirm it first," Dan said. But he was all smiles.

They got off at the fourth floor and walked to a large, well-lit room that looked like a science lab. Next to the door was a window with a small sliding panel beneath it.

"We can't go in," Dan explained. He rang the buzzer, placed the lock in a paper bag, then placed it into the sliding panel, along with some paperwork. "Call me when he's got a preliminary report, would you?" Dan asked the technician behind the glass, who nodded.

"What now?" Greg asked.

"Now? Dinner, of course. Have you eaten?" Dan asked.

The men took a stroll down to the Custom House, one of the oldest buildings in Norfolk. They turned onto

Granby and quickly found a small sandwich shop with a variety of fresh soups and salads. Greg could hardly contain his excitement and glanced at his watch frequently, but Dan managed to distract him. The agent speculated about the prospects for the Norfolk Tides, a Triple A ball club whose stadium was only minutes south of them.

By the time they made their way back to Dan's office, it was getting dark. Dan flipped on the office light and picked up his phone. In a few minutes he had checked his voice mail, jotted some notes, and hung up. He smiled broadly.

"We got a match on the gate lock with some shavings from a metal file. And the boots we found match the print found by the body. It's enough to make an arrest," he announced.

"Who's the lucky guy?" Greg asked.

"Win, place, and show," Dan said.

"Earl," Greg guessed correctly.

"Left the evidence in his truck." Dan beamed. "What a moron!"

Chapter Twenty-four

"You want to cover the rear?" Dan asked as he pulled into the parking lot of the Chesapeake Conservancy behind a Great Bridge sheriff's vehicle.

Greg nodded but with little enthusiasm. After all their work, it was a bit of a letdown to watch the local authorities serve the warrant for Earl Thompson's arrest on murder charges. But everyone had agreed, especially Floyd, who had talked with the mayor of Great Bridge personally. Dan and Greg would back up the sheriff's department. Theirs would be a secondary role. Mayor Greeley wanted the limelight on this one.

"Cheer up. You still have poachers to catch in the swamp, from what you tell me," Dan assured him.

"And the occasional moonshiner," Greg added.

"See? It's not all bad. Let's move."

Greg walked around to the back of the building as Dan and the two deputies entered the front. They had agreed that Dan would come out the back to get him once Thompson was in custody. Earl's truck was parked in the back, close to the rear entrance, so they knew he was inside. Carol, the office manager, had also phoned them once Earl arrived that morning. Greg yawned and cracked his knuckles as he paced by the door. His back was turned when he heard it begin to swing open.

"Let's get out of here," he said as he turned to greet Dan. But it was Earl's massive frame that filled the doorway. Greg jumped back a foot before he recovered his senses and reached for his weapon. When Earl saw that Greg was between him and his truck, he lowered his head and charged.

Greg had only a fraction of a second to pull the gun from his holster and was tackled as he raised the weapon in his outstretched arm. He hit the asphalt beneath the full weight of Earl. Greg couldn't breathe, as the wind was knocked out of him, but adrenaline was rushing through his veins. To his horror, when he hit the ground, he lost control of his weapon. He heard it slide across the pavement, and, at the same time, Earl pushed off Greg's chest to launch his desperate flight.

It wasn't his entire life that flashed before Greg's eyes in the next few seconds, just one small segment. Had he checked the box to buy life insurance when he applied for his job? He couldn't remember, but it suddenly seemed significant, with a mother depending on him for support. Life insurance would pay a lot of bills and for a lot of expensive drugs for her arthritis. Had he bought it? And then there was the humiliation factor—his brief success, then a legacy marked by the murmurs of friends and fellow officers at his funeral, saying, "Poor kid, shot with his own gun. Never should have let his guard down."

Greg rolled over but couldn't spot his gun as he saw Earl climb into the cab of his truck on the passenger side and slide into the driver's seat. Greg tried to stand but still searched for the breath that had been knocked from his lungs. Without it, he hadn't the strength to move. He made it to one knee before Dan swept by him, nearly knocking him back to the ground. Dan pulled open the passenger door of the truck and leveled his weapon at Earl.

"Take your hands off the wheel! Take 'em off! You turn that key, and I'll shoot!" he yelled. For a moment Earl stared, wild-eyed, at the man pointing a gun into his face before his arms dropped from the wheel.

"Come this way, toward me. Out of the cab!" Dan shouted. When Earl got out, Dan ordered him to turn around and put his hands on the roof. By that time, Greg was on his feet and had his cuffs in his left hand. He secured Earl, and seconds later the sheriff's deputies were escorting him to their patrol car. Dan watched them for a moment and then turned to say something to Greg, who was reaching under the front left tire of Earl's truck.

"Lose something?" he asked as Greg pulled his

weapon from beneath the truck. Greg was red-faced as he put his gun back into its holster.

"Just a word of advice. I'd hang on to that if I were you," Dan said good-naturedly.

Greg just muttered and followed the agent back to his car. He pulled the door shut, and his head fell to his chest as he realized anew that he could have easily just been killed. He was mulling this over when he realized that they were not moving and that Dan was staring at him.

"What?" Greg asked.

"So, what happened?" Dan asked in a hard tone of voice.

Greg sensed he was about to get a lecture on the proper handling of firearms, but in light of what had transpired, he could hardly object.

"I—I wasn't expecting Earl to come through the door. He caught me off guard. I didn't have time to draw my weapon," he admitted.

"You did train for this position, didn't you?" Dan asked.

"Of course I did," Greg protested. He looked out the window, angry but unable to think of anything to say. "You can bet it won't happen again," he muttered.

There was a silence that seemed very long to Greg before Dan spoke.

"I'm sure it won't, or it will definitely be the last time it happens. You were lucky." Then he started the car and gave Greg a gentle punch to the shoulder. "At least you slowed him down for me. Thanks! I wanted credit for the arrest anyway," he said.

"You're not welcome," Greg said slowly and emphatically.

A sly smile appeared across Dan's face as he put the car into gear.

Chapter Twenty-five

"Phone call for you," Cindy said as she stuck her head into the doorway and then popped out again.

Greg picked up the receiver and hit line two with his right hand, still cradling a report in his left. He was proofreading the final draft of the report on Ashley Myrtle's murder. He planned to give it to Floyd, who was due back from Florida the day after tomorrow.

"Greg Parnell. May I help you?" he asked.

"Agent Parnell, it's Carol."

"Carol?" He had a brief moment when he couldn't remember the association, but he didn't say so right away, because her voice held a ripe sense of sadness. He didn't want to offend her by confessing his ignorance.

"From the Conservancy."

Then the memory flooded back. "Oh, yes, of course.

What can I do for you?" Greg asked, sincerely empathetic. These types of calls could be very difficult.

"Some of us at the office wanted to visit the place where Ashley—well, you know. We wanted to leave some flowers and have a sort of private ceremony, if that would be okay."

Greg breathed a silent sigh of relief. This, at least, was within his power to grant. "Sure, that'd be fine. You must need directions? It's just off the northern end of the Jericho Ditch, about a hundred yards east into the woods. There's a wooden bridge that crosses the canal from the trail and takes you into the swamp," he explained. "I could take you there myself," he offered.

"Oh, that's nice of you to offer, but I'm not sure when we'd be able to organize everyone. You see, some of the volunteers want to go too, so I'm not sure if we'll try for tomorrow or the next day. But I understand cars aren't permitted. Can we get permission to drive in, at least to the bridge? We could walk the rest of the way."

"Certainly," Greg said. "Just come to the refuge headquarters, and I'll have a permit waiting for you. If I'm not here, ask for Cindy. I'll leave it with her, and she can answer any questions for you, provide maps, that sort of thing."

"Thank you," she said, the relief evident in her voice. "I don't think some of the people who want to make the trip are prepared for a long hike in the woods. Oh, and one more thing. We need the combination to the lock at the Jericho entrance. Unfortunately, Earl was the only one who knew the combination, and we can't find it written down anywhere. I certainly didn't want to contact him in jail, after all," she explained.

"I understand. No problem. I'll have that waiting for you as well, but Cindy knows it also. Is there anything else I can do for you?" Greg asked.

"No, except I wanted to say thank you, from all of us. It was quite a shock to discover that Earl was the one, but I'm glad that her murder was solved. It makes us feel a little easier here at the Conservancy."

"Just doing my job. I wish I could say it was a happy ending, but at least no one else will have to suffer."

"That's true. Well, thanks again."

"Good luck," Greg added before he hung up the phone. He was glad he could offer some assistance. He began reading the report again but stopped after a couple of minutes. He thought, or perhaps only felt, that he had forgotten something while he was talking to Carol. He couldn't put the feeling out of his mind but couldn't quite figure out what it was. No matter. Either he or Cindy would be here when her group arrived, and either could ensure that the group had all they needed.

He stepped out of Floyd's office and asked Cindy for the permit form, filled it out, and explained who it was for, and he wrote the combination for the gate lock on the back of the permit. After finishing the task, he tapped the form with his pen several times, deep in thought.

"Anything else?" Cindy finally asked.

"That's just what I was wondering," Greg confessed.

Cindy shook her head. "I can't think of anything. I'll

make sure they get this and some maps," she reassured him with a smile. "You can stop worrying."

"Okay, that's it then," he replied, and he smiled back. He was glad he had someone so organized and experienced to back him up, and he finally let the nagging doubt slip from his mind.

He returned to his report and finished reviewing it. Once he was done, he left it on the desk, where Floyd would be sure to see it, and prepared to leave. Perhaps now he could turn his attention to something less draining, like chasing poachers or confronting drug runners. At least, that part of his job was a little less traumatic. He flipped off the light and was headed out the door when the phone rang. He thought about letting it go, but a glance at his watch told him that he was still on duty for three more minutes, and he reluctantly picked up the receiver and flipped on the light.

"Great Dismal Swamp Refuge," he said.

"Hey, mountain man! Glad I caught you before you left. I think congratulations are in order," the voice said with great enthusiasm.

"Thanks, Dan," Greg replied. "Although the FBI helped a little."

"Just a little?" Special Agent Brennan asked.

"Just a bit."

"Well, let me see if this helps a little more. Dinner at the Locks Point. This case ending calls for a celebration."

"The Locks? Hmm, I don't know," Greg began. The Locks Point at Great Bridge was the town's finest restaurant, on the Intracoastal Waterway at Battlefield

Boulevard. Diners could watch a fleet of yachts, fishing boats, and sailing craft make their way through the canal while feasting on fresh fish caught locally. The food was excellent. It was also out of Greg's price range.

"Now, before you tell me you have to chase some poachers or look for a lost puppy in the woods, let me add three little words: Dinner's on me."

"What time?" Greg asked without hesitation.

"I thought you'd like that. See you in thirty minutes."

Twenty-eight minutes later, Greg pulled into the parking lot of the Locks Point at Great Bridge and parked his Corolla in an empty space close to the water. Already two boats were taking up position for the run through the lock, even though the bridge wouldn't open for another thirty minutes. Rather than a split span that rose up in two, the bridge was an old-fashioned turret, which turned on a center concrete pier to allow boats to pass, those headed north on the right and south on the left. The gatekeeper used hydraulic cranks to operate the span and started the process by hand, timed by only a simple glance at his wristwatch. This relic from earlier times was destined to be replaced sometime in the next few years by a multilane bridge, computer controlled and completely modernized. It would cost the gatekeeper his job, but since he was seventy-seven years old, he probably wouldn't mind by then. Greg waved to the man, who looked up from his paper in the lock office and waved back.

Greg headed into the restaurant and found Dan studying a Civil War–era map of Great Bridge while he nursed a drink at the bar. During that fateful period, which old-timers still referred to as The War of Northern Aggression, the locks at Great Bridge—and the Dismal Swamp Canal below—had both been destroyed. It was an effort by the Union Army and Navy to cut off supplies from the southern farmlands of North Carolina and starve Norfolk County into submission. No sign of hunger greeted anyone here, however.

Dan shook Greg's hand as he entered the bar and signaled to the bartender for a drink. "What ya have? Beer? Yuengling for my friend here," Dan ordered. Just then, they heard the hostess call them to their table. They carried their drinks into the dining area and sat by a window overlooking the locks.

"Enjoy your meal, officers," the hostess said warmly.

"Nice view," Greg observed.

"I thought you'd like it," Dan said as he picked up a menu. "I highly recommend the crab cakes, if you haven't had them here yet. They don't use any filler."

Greg whistled as his eyes moved across the pages of the menu. "I haven't had anything here ever," he confessed.

A waiter in a spotless white coat and black tie poured ice water into a crystal goblet in front of him and did the same for Dan.

"You should come here once in a while. Nice place to bring your girlfriend," Dan said. "Unless she prefers to slaughter her own food before she eats it. I know you outdoor types are fond of being self-reliant," he added.

"Very funny. I'd come here, but I can't afford it,"

Greg said. He didn't mention the woman on his mind who might enjoy a night at a place like this. Amanda. But it was the mounting medical bills from another woman, his mother, that kept him out of places like this. He didn't mention that either.

The waitress came and took their orders. Greg opted for the crab cakes, and Dan ordered a whole lobster with asparagus spears. Greg could only speculate at the price and shivered slightly at the term *Market Price* on the menu where a dollar amount should have been. Outside, at the water's edge, a great blue heron stabbed its bill into the water with a lightning thrust and pulled it out with a struggling fish at the tip.

"Looks like he got his for free," Dan laughed. Then he pulled a folded newspaper from his suit pocket and tossed it onto the white linen tablecloth. His finger stabbed the headline. "Did you see this?" The headline was from the local edition of that day's *Virginian-Pilot,* and read, "Arrest Made in Dismal Swamp Murder."

"Yeah, I saw it this morning. Cindy already had a copy tacked to the bulletin board when I got into work," Greg announced. The pride was evident in his voice.

"They even spelled your name right. That's always good. Wonder if that means the end of Ashley Myrtle's organization, tainted by scandal and all," Dan mused.

"Oh, I'm sure they'll survive. They're planning a memorial for her. It might even help them raise more money for their cause, as morose as that sounds."

"Well, I'm sure Mrs. Myrtle would have wanted it to go on, even without her," Dan said.

"You know, it's funny. Carol called me today. She wanted to leave some flowers at the murder site—she and some of the other workers at the Conservancy."

"Did they want you to go with them?"

"No. Believe it or not, she only wanted the combination for the gate. No one knew it except Earl, and she wasn't about to ask him for it. Strange, don't you think?"

Dan shook his head. "Not really."

"How so?"

"Power. He knew something they didn't, and he kept it to himself, so they'd be dependent on him. Probably knew lots of little stuff that he didn't share so he'd always be the 'go to' guy. It made him feel important."

Greg thought about that for a moment and finally nodded his agreement. "I suppose you're right," he said. "That was bothering me for a while. Something about it just didn't seem right. Maybe that's the explanation."

"Sure it is," Dan said. He raised his glass. "A toast. To Ashley Myrtle . . . may she rest in peace, and to Earl Thompson . . . may he rest in his cell, if not his grave, for a long, long time."

"Amen to that," Greg said, and he clinked his glass with Dan's.

The food was even better than Greg had imagined. It even pushed aside the warm smell of homemade spaghetti sauce that greeted him when he arrived home. For once, he'd be glad to enjoy it as leftovers the next day.

"Greg! I made a treat to celebrate," his mother said. Every milestone or successful case her son worked on was a tasty excuse for homemade spaghetti sauce cooked with meatballs and pork. She was disappointed when she heard his explanation as to why he wouldn't be eating.

"At least it will keep," she said. "I'm going to eat anyway, since I didn't have dinner yet. There's plenty for the rest of the week."

"I'll tell you what I would like. That sauce recipe. I want to sell it someday for a million dollars," he teased her.

"Sure, but I don't think it's worth it. Besides, it's not written down."

"What?" Greg asked in surprise. "How do you know what to put in it? I thought you said that was your grandmother's secret recipe."

"It is. Grandma taught it to my mother, and she passed it on to me. I'll teach it to you, and you can pass it down to your kids."

Despite his full stomach, Greg couldn't resist putting a meatball and some sauce onto a small plate and joining her at the table.

"I knew you'd have some. Good as always?"

"Absolutely. But how do you make sure it always comes out right if it's not written down?"

"Honey, some things you never forget. Once you learn this recipe and make it yourself, it'll stay with you forever. It's like riding a bike. You won't have to write it down. The right combination of ingredients will stay in your head."

Greg smiled, nodded, and then froze. He swallowed a mouthful. "What did you say?" he asked.

"It's like riding a bike," she offered.

"No, after that," he demanded.

"What? All I said was the combination of ingredients—"

"That's it!" he remarked, and he smacked his forehead.

"Of course that's it," she concurred. "Use the right combination of ingredients."

"No. The combination! To the gate at Washington Ditch!" he said, and he stood up so abruptly that his chair tumbled to the kitchen floor. "Earl wouldn't have tried to break the lock. He knew the combination. Mom, you're a genius!" he said. He leaned over and kissed her.

She smiled. "I could have told you that," she said nonchalantly.

"But don't you see what this means?" he asked grimly.

"You want some spaghetti after all?"

"No. I'm afraid it means that we may still have a murderer on the loose."

Chapter Twenty-six

"What are those for?" the guard asked Greg after inspecting the box of Timberland boots, size 11½. "He can't wear those. They're not prison-issue."

"Just a little experiment. I promise I won't be leaving them behind," Greg assured him.

"Okay, wait here. He'll be out in a few minutes." The guard left, but Greg knew he would be just outside the door, watching. The visitors' room consisted of a long table with three chairs on each side, and a small wooden frame, three inches high, down the center of the table, which separated the visitor from the prisoner. The walls were in need of paint, the ivory color yellowed by age. On the floor, scuff marks and deposits of gum gave the room a dingy quality, made worse by the exposed fluorescent lightbulbs that sent a sharp glare into the air. Greg would be glad to leave this place as soon as possible.

The door across the room opened on creaky hinges, and a guard escorted Earl Thompson into the room. He was handcuffed and shackled, which was a little unusual. Greg speculated that he had been giving the guards some trouble and had earned the jail jewelry as a reward for his behavior. It quickly became apparent that his behavior hadn't improved.

"What do you want?" he said with disgust dripping from his lips after he sat down. He plopped his hands onto the table with a heavy clank.

"I wanted to ask you a couple of questions, that's all," Greg said.

"My lawyer doesn't want me talking to anyone, and I certainly don't want to talk to you. I told you, I didn't kill Ashley."

Greg studied him for a moment. "How would you feel if I told you that I might not be satisfied with some loose ends in this case, and that it might help you to answer a few questions?"

Now it was Earl's turn to eye Greg. "What is this, some sort of trick? You trying to trick me?" he asked warily.

"Not at all," Greg assured him. "I just want to ask you one thing, something that you already know the answer to. I just want to be sure."

"Forget it."

"Look, I'll just ask. You don't have to answer until you check with your lawyer."

"What's the question?" Earl finally asked after a long pause.

"What's the combination to the gate at Washington Ditch?"

Earl's eyes narrowed to dark slits. "Why should I answer that? You're just trying to put me there the day of the murder, aren't you?" he asked suspiciously.

"Not at all. Carol called me. She wanted the combination so she could leave flowers at the spot where Ashley died. She mentioned that you were the only one in the office who knew the combination. You used it all the time to do fieldwork in the Dismal Swamp. You told me yourself, at our first interview. It's in my notes. I just want to know if she was right. It made me wonder why you would try to file through the lock if you knew the combination."

Earl hesitated, then said, "Sure, why not? Everyone in that office was aware I went there to do research. The combo is 34, 3, 18."

Greg smiled. "Is that your final answer?" he asked. Earl did not appear amused. "Anyway, that's correct," Greg said, as they both knew.

"So, you agree I'm innocent?" Earl asked, leaning forward so suddenly that the guard stiffened and leaned forward as well.

"I didn't say that," Greg reminded him. "I just said I was trying to tie up some loose ends that don't seem to fit together." Greg allowed his gaze to drop down to the box he had placed at his feet, on his side of the table, and he felt Earl follow the action.

"What's in the box?" Earl asked.

"My resignation, if I'm not right," Greg quipped.

"What are you babbling about?"

"Nothing," Greg said. He opened the box and pulled out the right boot.

"Timberlands, like the pair found in your truck."

"I told you, those aren't mine. Mine are in my office. I only wear them when I'm doing fieldwork."

"I know. We found them. Of course, you could have more than one pair. I just wanted to see if these fit." Greg glanced at the guard. "Okay if he tries this on?" The guard nodded.

"Take a hike," Earl replied. He turned toward the guard and asked, "Can I get back to my cell? It's almost time for Oprah Winfrey."

"Are you sure you don't want to try them on? They're your size. Eleven and a half."

"That proves they're not mine," Earl said.

"How will you know until you try them on?"

"Because I wear a size thirteen!" Earl declared triumphantly.

"Really?"

"That's it. Talk to my lawyer," he said, and he stood to head for his cell. "You're trying to frame me. Well, it's not gonna work!" he bellowed.

"Take it easy," Greg urged, but a moment later Earl was gone. Greg picked up the boots and headed for his car. At least now he knew that the boots found in Earl's truck were the wrong size. *Perhaps*, he thought, *Earl was telling the truth*. And since he knew the combination for the lock at the Washington Ditch gate, Earl wouldn't have to file it off.

It was beginning to look as if another person had been in the Dismal Swamp that day, driving Earl's truck. Driving his truck and maybe murdering Ashley Myrtle. He couldn't wait to run this theory past Dan. If Earl knew what he was really thinking, he'd be shaking Greg's hand. But he needed proof. Those loose ends still didn't fit together.

Chapter Twenty-seven

Agent Brennan's voice answered after five rings, a time lapse that seemed like an eternity to Greg. He suspected that he would meet resistance when he told Dan that the wrong man might be in custody.

"Brennan here," the voice confirmed. He sounded tired.

Greg froze for a moment,

"Hello?" the voice asked in a sharp tone.

"Hey, Dan," Greg said. He was still thinking fast about his reply.

"Greg? What can I do for you? Did you take your girlfriend to that restaurant yet?" he asked, referring to Locks Point, where they had celebrated.

"Not yet," Greg admitted. "But I did want to see if I could ask you for a favor," he added with a little trepidation.

"Sure, sure, buddy," Dan said quickly. "You need something, you got it," he confirmed.

"I'm writing a report for my boss on the Ashley Myrtle case, and I could use a copy of the inventory we seized from Earl Thompson's house and truck," Greg said.

"No problem. I can make a copy and fax it to you."

"That works, but actually I'm going to be in Norfolk today," Greg said, "and I thought I could pick it up around noon or so."

"Uh, that's good. Wanna do lunch? There's some good eats at the Waterside," Dan added, referring to the waterfront building that overlooked Norfolk Harbor just north of the midtown tunnel.

A food court had moved into the building and had given the dying businesses a new lease on life. This was due in no small part to the cheaper leases the city had been willing to write to preserve their survival. New tenants had helped as well. Jillian's, a combination game arcade with a bar and grill, had moved in and taken over most of the second level of the two-story building. This business, along with a new disco dance club playing '70s music for young couples who had only dim memories of that decade, were drawing bigger crowds at night. During the day, office professionals could choose from a number of casual dining restaurants that overlooked the water.

Greg was familiar with the area. "That sounds good," he agreed.

"Okay, meet me at the Bank of America ATM on

Main Street. I have to pick up some cash, and then we'll walk over to Waterside."

Greg headed out the door and waved at Cindy, who was passing out assignments to some of the staff.

"Hey, nice job on that Myrtle case," Brad commented.

"Congratulations," Sarah added.

"Don't congratulate me just yet," Greg warned with a smile.

"You're being modest," Sarah teased.

"I wish," Greg said with more grimness than he wanted to convey. "I'm headed to Norfolk for an appointment, Cindy," he called over his shoulder as he exited the front door.

Greg found Dan at the bank forty minutes later. Dan glanced at his watch, a signal that Greg understood.

"Sorry. The midtown bridge opened," Greg said.

"Yeah, I saw that ship—a battle cruiser, I think—go by about ten minutes ago. Around here you can never make plans to be anywhere without getting caught by a drawbridge sooner or later." They headed down Water Street, and Dan pulled two folded sheets of paper from his coat pocket.

"Here ya go," he said, handing them to Greg.

"Thanks," Greg said. "You been on the *Wisconsin* yet?" he asked, and he pointed to the decommissioned warship visible at the end of Main Street, docked next to a marine museum.

"Of course," Dan replied. "She's a beauty. One of my buddies, just retired from the Navy, served aboard her in the Gulf War. You're not allowed belowdecks, but he fixed it so I could have the grand tour. You?"

"Naw, not yet. I've been meaning to but haven't found the time."

"Greg, my boy, we've got to get you out more. They've opened six new restaurants on Granby Street alone this year."

"And I bet you've been to every one of them," Greg said.

Dan raised his chin in the air and ran the tips of three fingers through his hair before he said, "Yes, well, just doing my part to keep the ladies from getting too lonely at night."

They crossed the street past a colorful metal sculpture of a mermaid that welcomed visitors to the Waterside and entered the building. A kaleidoscope of scents greeted them. Some came from the food purveyors, others from a candle shop just inside the building.

"Jillian's is good, but they take forever at lunchtime. Too crowded," Dan said. "Let's stay down here. What's your pleasure? Steak sandwiches, pizza, seafood? Joe's Crab Shack has a nice lunch. You like Thai?"

"Never had it," Greg said.

"There's a good one here. Let's try that. If you like spicy food, this is the place."

"Okay."

They got their food and sat near a raised platform on which a piano player entertained the crowd with a selection of light jazz tunes.

Greg took a bite of noodles. Dan was about to ask

Greg what he thought but heard a quick intake of breath and saw Greg quickly reach for his iced tea.

"Not bad, huh?" Dan said with a grin as he bravely took another bite of his own food.

"Excellent," Greg admitted, although he dabbed his forehead, beaded with sweat, with his handkerchief. The men ate in silence for a few minutes. Greg examined the inventory list while Dan concentrated on his food, interrupted by a glance at one or two women strolling past the piano player.

"So, you got everything you need?" Dan asked finally.

Greg scowled. "It's a funny thing. . . ." he began.

"The boots?" Dan interjected.

Greg appeared surprised. "You noticed too?"

Dan, his mouth full of food, simply nodded.

"Doesn't that seem suspicious to you?"

"Not really," Dan said. "He could have picked up the wrong pair when he bought them, or gotten them on sale so cheap, he figured he'd make do with a tight fit, or something."

"Yeah, you're probably right," Greg said with a confidence he did not truly feel. "There's probably a good explanation for that other thing too," he added, and he returned to his food. A moment later Dan's reply confirmed that Greg's offhand comment had hit home.

"What 'other thing'?" Dan asked, saying the words slowly and with a hint of irritation.

"Huh?" Greg asked, feigning ignorance.

"The 'other thing'?" Dan repeated.

"Oh, yeah," Greg said, and he thrust a plastic fork

into the air. "That thing, you know, about the gate lock." He quickly returned to his food.

"Why don't you tell me, sort of refresh my memory?" Dan said. He folded his hands in his lap and leaned back in his chair.

"Well," Greg said, swallowing a slug of iced tea, "I'm sure you do studies of criminals—profiles, that sort of thing—at the FBI. There's probably some theory that explains why Earl Thompson just completely forgot the combination to the gate at Washington Ditch. I mean, after all, he just killed a woman, one he'd been obsessing about. It could have thrown him into shock. It just seems sort of odd, you know, to the untrained eye."

Dan stared at him for a moment. Greg was beginning to hope he was persuading the agent.

"I did study criminal profiling during my training, but I'm far from an expert," Dan conceded. "But I don't have to be an expert to see that you're trying to convince me of some theory you've decided to embrace, namely, that you think Earl Thompson may not be the murderer. But instead of saying so, you're trying to pull some psychological wool over my eyes so I'll suddenly jump up and say 'Oh, my! We have the wrong man!' You never miss an opportunity to find something wrong with this case. How's that for profiling?" Dan asked. His eyebrows squeezed together, and he glared at Greg.

"Was it that obvious?" Greg asked, a hint of disappointment in his voice.

Dan smiled and nodded. "Besides, how do you know he couldn't remember the combination? He left by the Jericho Ditch gate, which was unlocked, not by the Washington Ditch gate," Dan reminded him.

"Remember my witness, the bird-watcher?" Greg asked.

"Yeah, I remember. The witness saw Thompson. Earl looked up and saw him, so he took off. He left because he didn't want to be identified, not because he couldn't get the gate opened."

"What about the file?"

"What about it?" Dan asked. He pulled their empty plates onto the tray and headed for a trash bin, trailed by Greg.

"The file we pulled from Earl's truck, with the metal shavings on it," Greg reminded him. "Your lab said the shavings matched the metal of the combination lock at Washington Ditch."

"Lemme see that," Dan said as he turned and thrust out a hand.

Greg gave them to him and pointed to the bottom of the first page. "See? Right here. That was one of the key pieces of evidence mentioned in securing the arrest warrant, along with the boots."

Dan shook his head. "That just confirms that he was there. This makes it worse for him," Dan objected.

"It proves the file was there, and the truck, but not that Earl drove it that day," Greg said emphatically.

"Oh, for Pete's sake," Dan said, and he waved a hand and walked away, pushing the inventory list back at Greg. Greg followed him out the door into the sunshine.

"You know what? You sound like his lawyer! Maybe

you should defend him," Dan said with sarcasm. A couple walking into the Waterside stepped aside and stared at the two agents as they made their way to the street corner.

"Remember when I told you over dinner that Carol called me and asked if her group could visit the site where Ashley's body was found?" Greg asked. "She needed the combination to the gate so they could drive there. She said that Earl was the only one at the Conservancy who knew the combination. Since he knew the combination, he didn't have to try to break it open. Earl wasn't in the swamp that day. Ashley simply borrowed Earl's truck, just like he said. Ashley went there with someone else, and whoever it was, he killed her in the swamp and then tried to get out by taking a shortcut to the Washington Ditch. But the gate was locked. That's when he tried to file it off. He saw my witness and fled, heading back to the only gate that was unlocked, the one they had come in at Jericho."

The light changed to green, and several pedestrians began to cross, but Dan simply stood there on the corner, staring across the street. His face, which had been angry, slowly relaxed, and his mouth dropped. He turned to Greg and held out his hand wordlessly for the inventory. He looked it over again, this time more slowly, then handed it back. He pulled out a notebook and flipped through it. Finally he spoke, one finger pressed to a page.

"Your witness didn't positively identify Earl Thompson as the man he saw that day, did he?" Dan asked.

"No, he was too far away. But he did say the truck

was white and had a green logo on the door, similar to the one used by the Conservancy," Greg reminded him. Dan flipped the notebook closed and began to cross the street. The light changed to red and forced him to stop at the concrete island halfway across, with Greg still on his heels.

"Interesting," Dan finally conceded, "but it's not enough to reopen the case."

"Bull!" Greg exploded, seizing on the small admission. It was the wrong tactic, because Dan suddenly backed away.

"You know, this isn't the first time you've gone down this path," Dan said. "I did a little research too. You seem to have a history of following cases after they've been closed. Isn't that right, Lieutenant Parnell, US Army with the military police?"

Greg was startled but quickly recovered before his face gave him away. "Checking up on me, huh? That's your game now?" he asked in a tone that was a challenge instead of a question.

The light changed, and they crossed the street. "Just standard operating procedure, my boy," Dan announced. "This theory you have, about the wrong man being arrested, is getting to be a bad habit with you. In fact, isn't that why you had to leave the Army?" he asked, a smirk hidden just behind his lips.

They paused at the next corner. Greg resisted the urge to plant a fist right in the middle of the agent's smug face. Instead, he leaned close to him and planted his eyes on Dan's. Dan backed away as Greg inched his body slowly next to him until the buttons on Greg's uniform clicked against Dan's suit buttons.

"What are you doing? I'm not a fan of close encounters, and I can take you anytime," Dan warned, and he placed an open hand on Greg's shoulder.

"Maybe you should complete your research. When you do, you might find out that my 'theory,' as you put it, was the only thing that kept an innocent Army private from a close encounter with a gurney and a needle in his arm," Greg said angrily. He turned and walked back toward the city parking lot, in the opposite direction from which Dan had come. He heard the agent call out to him but refused to slow his pace. Greg yelled two short words back over his shoulder, the first of which was not *Happy* and the second of which was not *Birthday*.

Chapter Twenty-eight

Greg walked through his front door and flopped down on the couch. He was exhausted and now felt confused as well. He picked up the phone after twenty minutes and called the refuge to tell Cindy he would not be in for the rest of the day. He had to think, to decide if perhaps Dan was right and he was seeing something that wasn't there.

He had barely hung up when the phone rang. It was Cindy.

"Sorry, Greg. But I forgot to tell you that Dan Brennan called," she explained.

"Dan? I just had lunch with him."

"Actually, he called twice in the last twenty minutes. He said it was important, so I gave him your number at home. Is that okay?" she asked.

"Sure, that's fine," Greg lied. It was too late to do anything about it now. "What did he want?"

"He wants you to meet him at the Courtyard Café at four o'clock for coffee. He said it's about the combination lock. Maybe he wants to return it," she suggested.

"Fine, I'll meet him. Call him back and tell him," he said. After he hung up, he began to doze, and he went to his room to set his alarm for three-thirty. Whatever Dan wanted, and he suspected it wasn't to return a piece of evidence, he needed some rest. He closed his eyes and had barely dropped onto the bed, it seemed, when the buzzer went off. He changed his shirt and combed his hair before he headed out the door.

The Courtyard Café was on the corner of Johnstown Road and Battlefield Boulevard, and Greg reached the restaurant in just a few minutes. He was early, but he saw Dan as soon as he entered.

"What do you want?" Greg asked when he approached the table.

"Have a seat," Dan offered, pointing to a chair.

"What's up? Didn't you get enough insults in?" Greg asked sarcastically.

"Suppose I said," Dan began, "that you weren't the only one who noticed a discrepancy in the evidence?"

"I'd say there was someone in the FBI who was smarter than you," Greg said as he reluctantly sat down, "which doesn't surprise me at all."

Dan smiled grimly. "Along with the tidbits you pointed out to me, it seems that someone noticed that there were no fingerprints found on the rearview mirror of Earl's truck—not even Earl's. Now, why would a suspect remove fingerprints from his own vehicle?"

"He wouldn't," Greg said, betraying his excitement when he leaned across the table.

"Well, you're going to get your wish. Brian, my supervisor, wants me to ask a few more questions, clear up some loose ends without arousing any suspicions. And he wants me to bring you along," Dan said.

"Now you're talking," Greg replied.

"Just don't let it go to your head. You haven't proved anything yet," Dan remarked, and he got up from the table. They entered the parking lot, and before Greg could open his mouth, Dan blurted, "I'll drive."

After a few minutes Greg asked, "Where are we going?"

"I'd like to talk to that Councilman Myrtle again. But our first stop is back to chat with William Meyers. Let's see if we can clear up that discrepancy about the lunch appointment. And maybe we can find out if he knew that Ashley was going to shut him down."

"Meyers did have the simplest motive—money. Do you still have the search warrant?" Greg inquired.

"No. It expired anyway, but even if it hadn't, I wouldn't use it. Subtle, remember? Let's be nice and friendly."

"Friendly? Maybe we should take him to dinner," Greg joked.

"Looks like they beat us to the punch," Dan remarked. They pulled up to the Meyers' driveway just as Bill and his wife were emerging, dressed for an evening out on the town. Bill wore a dark-gray three-piece suit with a watch chain in his vest pocket. Crystal wore a purple gown with silk sleeves and a midthigh slit in the side. Her black heels added two inches to her thin figure, which was accented by the clinging material of her dress. A gold brooch on her shoulder caught the rays of the setting sun and sparkled like a diamond. It was topped by a small violet flower.

"What a lovely couple!" Greg exclaimed as they emerged from Dan's car. "Looks like we caught you at a bad time."

"We were just going into Norfolk for dinner and a play," Bill Meyers said. "Is there something we can do for you?"

"Actually, we just wanted to clear up a couple of loose ends," Dan said vaguely.

"Loose ends," Crystal repeated. "I thought you arrested the murderer."

"We did," Greg admitted. "But we're still gathering evidence, investigating for the DA. The trial may be several months away."

"That's right," Dan added, "and we just were wondering about a couple of things related to Thompson, the accused."

Bill looked a little put out by their arrival but relented. "Well, I suppose we can spare a few minutes, but then we'll have to be on our way. Won't you come in?" he offered.

Dan and Greg followed them into the foyer, which had a twelve-foot ceiling dominated by a crystal chandelier that threw streaks of light and color in every direction.

Bill reached for a tumbler off a small portable bar

and poured himself a scotch. "I'd offer you one, but I'm sure you gentlemen are on duty," he remarked. He took an unhealthy swig before asking, "What can I do for you?"

"Well, if you remember, you said you called Ashley Myrtle to see if she could have lunch with you because you were in the area. About what time was that?" Dan asked.

Greg noted that Crystal, who had sat down in a green love seat in the front parlor, suddenly stared at her husband. Bill didn't catch the look, distracted by Dan's question.

"Oh, I don't know, around eleven o'clock, maybe a little later. Is the time so important?" Bill asked, perplexed.

"It's just that Ashley had the lunch date written down in her appointment book. We found it in her office, you see. And usually, when someone makes spontaneous plans, they don't feel the need to write it down. I was wondering if it might have been a couple hours earlier?" Dan asked.

Meyers smiled. "Oh, I suppose it might have been a little earlier. It was a very hectic week, Special Agent Brennan. You understand," he said with a smile. But Greg noticed the shine of moisture on Bill's forehead. Crystal noticed too, and she sat forward stiffly on the edge of the love seat. Was he getting nervous or merely warm due to his suit and tie?

"Sometimes I make a note of an event afterward in my appointment book," Crystal suddenly said. This brought everyone's attention to the parlor and away from Bill, who pulled a handkerchief from his pocket and patted his forehead.

"How's that?" Dan asked. He hadn't expected any remark from Crystal Meyers, and it caught him off guard.

"Well, I get so busy, I sometimes fill in an appointment afterward so I have a record of it. Bill does too, don't you, dear? For tax purposes, I think you said."

"Yes, that's true," Bill concurred. "I'm sure Ashley keeps—uh, kept—very meticulous records. Was that all you needed?" he asked Dan, and he stepped toward the front door. Crystal rose from her seat and joined him. Her hand slipped under his arm.

"One other thing, Mr. Meyers. Do you recognize this?" Dan asked him, and he handed him a piece of paper. As Bill read the paper, Greg noticed that Dan shot him a nasty look.

"I don't think so. Should I?" Bill asked, and he passed it back to Dan.

"You don't recognize this number?" Dan asked again, and he passed the paper to Greg.

"No, and I'm not sure what this has to do with Earl Thompson and his vicious attack on Ashley," he protested.

"We just want to get all the facts straight, in case Earl's defense attorney tries to suggest that someone else was involved in her death. We wouldn't want to give him any openings, now would we? As for this number, maybe this will help refresh your memory," Dan remarked, and he pulled a copy of a cashier's check from his suit pocket and gave it to Bill. He stared at it for several seconds, as Crystal peered from his side.

"Oh, it's a lot number, for a piece of property. Isn't that right, dear?" Crystal asked with a glance up at her husband. "This is the lot number for the property that Bill bought so he could build Drummond Estates. Well, you can hardly expect him to remember such small details, Agent Brennan. After all, my husband has lawyers and accountants for that sort of thing," she announced cheerfully.

Bill patted her arm and added, "Thank you, darling, but I think I can explain it." Bill looked at Dan. "Satisfied?" he asked with a scratchy voice.

"It's just that this number was written next to her lunch appointment with you, and we concluded that she intended to talk to you about it. Did she?" Dan pressed.

"I already told you that we talked about work," Bill said. He was becoming agitated. "But not about my development specifically," he added.

"She didn't mention that she was going to recommend that Drummond Estates be shut down to protect the wetlands around it from being drained and destroyed?" Dan asked. This was his ace in the hole, and as he played it, he saw Bill's calm demeanor begin to crack.

"Oh, that's silly!" Crystal remarked. "Ashley's an old friend of the family. Why would she want to hurt us?" she asked, dismissing the idea with a casual toss of her left hand. But the fingers of her right hand tightened on Bill's arm, and the knuckles turned white.

"That's what we'd like to know. And, more specifically, if you knew about these plans," Dan said.

"My husband already told you that he didn't know anything about the wetlands report," Crystal said. "Besides, it was probably Earl's recommendation. His name was on it too."

"True enough," Greg said, speaking for the first time.

Dan glared at him again.

"Was there anything else, gentlemen?" Bill asked. "We really should be going if we want to keep our dinner plans."

"Did you have any questions?" Dan asked Greg, still glaring at him.

"Actually, I did," he announced. Everyone sighed.

"Where did you get that lovely piece of jewelry?" Greg asked, pointing to Crystal's pin.

For a moment Crystal looked surprised, and then a smile broke across her lips. "Oh, this? Do you like it?" she asked, touching the brooch. Greg approached for a closer look.

"I got it at Maxwell's in McArthur Mall, downtown Norfolk," she said proudly. "It was a gift from my husband."

"That is stunning. You know, I've been looking for something like this. Mother's Day is only a couple of months away," Greg said.

"How nice," Dan muttered.

"Wonderful," Bill declared with muted disgust.

"That flower looks so realistic, it's amazing," Greg remarked.

"Oh, it is real," Crystal replied.

"You're kidding. How can it be?"

"It's some sort of acrylic spray the jeweler uses," Crystal explained. "It preserves the flower and then hardens and can be attached to the gold."

"Wow. Do you think he could do this for me?"

"Oh, I'm sure he could. Just ask for Paul Maxwell. If you mention my name, I'm sure he'd remember making it."

"It's so delicate. I've never seen that flower before. You must have grown it in that lovely garden you have," Greg said.

"Actually, my husband gave it to me. He's such a romantic. Remember, honey? You had that flat tire last week, just before your trip to New York?" she asked her husband. She turned to address Greg before Bill could muster a reply. "I found him in the bathroom washing up. He was all dirty and muddy, and this flower was sticking out of his collar. Well, he told me about having to change the flat on his car, which explained why he looked a wreck. And when I asked him where he got the flower, he told me he was thinking of me and brought it home," she said, and she gazed up at him with loving eyes. "Can you believe I actually thought for just a moment that a woman had given it to him? How silly of me. Anyway, I took it to Maxwell the very next morning, and he suggested this treatment."

"That's great," Greg agreed. He looked at Bill and Crystal and said, "I'd like to get something like this

made. Where did you say you found it? The flower?"
Greg asked.

"Along Interstate 64, just a few miles east of here.
There were a lot of them. I'm sure they grow all along
the shoulders of the highway. You shouldn't have any
trouble finding some. Now, if that's all, we really must
be going," Bill said with a smile. He opened the door for
Greg and Dan and then pulled his wife out behind him.

"Thanks again," Greg said.

"No problem," Crystal said cheerfully.

"Hey, have you ever been into the Dismal Swamp
Refuge?" Greg asked them as he was stepping into
Dan's car. Bill and Crystal shook their heads. "Mr.
Meyers, not even once?"

"I'm afraid I haven't had the pleasure," he admitted
as he opened his car door.

"Well, give me a call. I'd be glad to arrange a personal
tour for you," Greg said, and he waved at the couple.

Crystal smiled and waved until Dan's car disappeared around a bend in the road. "I thought they'd
never leave," she said.

"Amen to that," Bill agreed. "Uh, darling, I think I'd
like to bring those opera glasses for the play. Excuse
me for a moment." Bill entered the house and went into
the library just past the parlor. That had been a close
call, and he had decided it was time to destroy the last
obstacle to his plans for Drummond Estates. It had
been foolish to hang on to it, but the paper shredder

would make short work of it. He reached behind the bookshelf and felt around with his fingers.

"It's not there," a voice declared. He spun around to see Crystal standing at the entrance to the library, her arms folded across her chest.

"I, uh, I thought they—but I suppose it doesn't matter," Bill said, fumbling for words.

"Oh, Bill, don't worry," Crystal said as she walked over to him. She placed her hands on his face and looked into his eyes. "I've taken care of it. They'll never find the report you hid behind that bookcase."

"You . . . you knew?" he said with astonishment.

"A good wife always knows her husband's mind," she said with a devious smile. "You didn't think I was going to let that report fall into the wrong hands, did you? Especially after you had the guts to shut her up for good."

"What?" Bill stammered. "Okay, I admit she gave me a copy of the report. But I had nothing to do with her death," he protested.

"Darling, relax," Crystal urged him, and she kissed his cheek. "Don't you know anything? Wives can't be forced to testify against their husbands. I'm sure you didn't plan to kill her." She took his hand and headed for the door. In the foyer she paused and adjusted her hair. "Besides, it's all for the best. She would have ruined everything, and you've got a lot of houses to build if you're going to make us rich. We'd better be going if we're going to eat before the play."

Bill followed his wife dutifully out of the house and,

for the first time in weeks, opened the car door for her. As she slid into the leather seat, he asked, "How can I ever thank you?"

She smiled to herself. "I'm sure I'll think of something," she replied.

Greg and Dan drove in silence until the car reached Battlefield Boulevard, where Dan pulled into the corner parking lot of a closed hardware store. He cut the engine, and for several seconds he simply stared incredulously at Greg.

"What was that all about?" he finally asked. "Jewelry? Mother's Day?"

"You said we should be friendly," Greg protested.

Dan dropped his head onto the steering wheel. "Saint Joseph, give me strength," he whispered. "Didn't you see me staring at you? I was trying to get your attention."

"Yeah, I noticed that," Greg admitted. "It was really irritating."

"I wanted you to question him!" Dan yelled. "He was sweating bullets! Don't tell me you missed that!"

"No, I noticed. He was pretty nervous, wasn't he?"

"Exactly!" Dan exclaimed, glad that at least one of his statements had sunk into Greg's head. "He was on the verge of breaking. If we had double-teamed him, we might have had him!" Dan said.

"Maybe. Maybe not," Greg suggested.

"Well, at least you could have tried," Dan demanded. "He was hiding something, something big. Frankly, I'm starting to think you were right about Earl, and maybe Bill's our man. But we missed our best chance. We'll never get a confession now."

"Actually, we got him already. And thanks, by the way, for admitting I was right."

Dan threw his arms up into the air. "Hey, you're very welcome. I must have missed something in there. Did he tell you that he killed Ashley Myrtle?"

"Nope. She did."

"Who?"

"Crystal, the wife."

Dan's mouth swung open so wide that Greg could see the man's back teeth. "Crystal told you?" he asked in disbelief.

"Yep."

"Could you please explain?"

"Sure, but it's getting late," Greg said, looking at his watch. "We're going to need a search warrant."

"Anything else?" Dan asked after a moment.

"Yeah, an arrest warrant would be nice."

"How are we going to convince a judge that we have probable cause for either of those two items?" Dan demanded.

"Start the car," Greg said, tapping a finger on the ignition. "I'll explain on the way."

Chapter Twenty-nine

It was after one in the morning when Bill opened the door to their house. "Boy, I'm bushed. That was a great play, though."

"How would you know? You slept through the third act," Crystal replied. "I wonder why there are so many cars on the street."

"Someone must be having a party," Bill replied. "Too bad we weren't invited," he joked. Crystal had barely closed the door, when a knock fell upon it.

Husband and wife looked at each other. "Maybe we were," Crystal said, and she opened the door.

"You!" Bill said. "What is it now? Can't this wait until morning?"

"If you haven't noticed," Greg said as he entered, "it is morning. This is a warrant to search the house," he announced, handing it to Bill. Three uniformed deputies streamed into the foyer and fanned out in different directions.

"And this," Dan said, "is a warrant for your arrest, for the murder of Ashley Myrtle."

"What? That's preposterous!" Bill said.

"Bill, don't say anything!" his wife urged. She turned to glare at Greg. "They don't have any proof. We'll be fine, as long as we keep our cool. My husband will not say another word without his lawyer," she announced. A thin smile broke upon her face. As if to confirm her confidence, Dan read Bill his Miranda rights.

"Actually, that's fine with me. We already have someone's testimony that confirms that your husband killed Mrs. Myrtle," Greg said.

"That's absurd. Whoever told you my husband killed Ashley is a devious liar."

"Well, you may be devious, but I don't think you were lying," Dan replied.

For a moment, Dan's statement flew over Crystal's head, but she quickly pulled it down. "Me? I said no such thing!" she blurted. Her face glowed crimson, and her hands shook.

"Yes, you did," Greg claimed. "Think, Mrs. Meyers. I'm sure it will come to you."

"Stop taunting her," Bill Meyers demanded as a sheriff placed a pair of handcuffs on the developer's arms.

"You're trying to trick me," Crystal said, her voice trembling. She sat down on the love seat in the parlor. Her head spun around to take in the movement of the ongoing search, the sight of her husband in handcuffs, the classic furniture, and the stately home they had built. "My things," she whispered. Then her face hardened. She stood up. "Earl Thompson killed Ashley. You said so," she reminded them.

"We did think so, even arrested him, that's true. But I soon changed my mind," Greg said.

"I, on the other hand, needed some convincing," Dan added. "You provided that tonight, although I didn't realize it until Greg explained it to me."

"How?" Crystal asked.

"When we were asking your husband about his lunch date with Ashley, you couldn't resist butting in. That's when you mentioned the report, the one that she wrote, which you insisted your husband had never seen. There was only one printed copy, and that was taken from her when she was killed. But you knew that Earl's name was on it, as Ashley's co-author. 'Earl's name was on it too,' you said. You couldn't have known that unless you had read it for yourself before you destroyed it," Greg explained.

Crystal laughed, or tried to, but the sound was garbled in her throat. "Oh, that? I was just guessing, that's all," she claimed.

"Well, that's for a jury to decide. But there's no guessing about this," he said, and he walked over to her and removed the brooch from her dress before she could stop him. He stepped out of reach as she grasped at the delicate flower.

"You didn't find this flower by the roadside," Greg said with disdain in his voice as he looked at Bill. "It's a dwarf trillium, one of the rarest flowers in North America. There's only one place you could have gotten it. Deep in the Dismal Swamp, a place you claimed you have never entered. You probably picked it up on your clothes after you murdered Ashley by smothering her in the mud of the swamp. Then you dumped her body in the Jericho canal, hoping it would look like an accidental drowning. I found a petal from this species of flower on her sleeve, and it led me back to the place where you killed her."

"My husband found that flower weeks ago, long before Ashley was killed," Crystal claimed.

"Weeks ago?" Greg asked, and he shook his head. "Not a chance. The dwarf trillium only blooms for a few days in the middle of March. At best, that was last week or the week before, not several weeks ago. And we've already spoken to your jeweler, since you were kind enough to give us his name. He, in turn, was kind enough to confirm that you brought the flower to him the day after Ashley disappeared. Any later, and it would have wilted. Your husband brought you that flower the same day he murdered Ashley in the Dismal Swamp."

"Mr. Maxwell wasn't very happy, being awakened at midnight, but he understood once we served him with a search warrant for your account records," Dan added.

A deputy interrupted long enough to show Greg a set of keys he was handling with rubber gloves. "They were behind the top row of books in the library," the deputy said

"Ashley's keys?" Greg asked Bill, who stared at him in silence. "You must have used these to get in and

delete her report from every computer in the Chesapeake Conservancy building."

"Took us a while, but we managed to recover the
files," Dan said proudly.

"I told you, she was a family friend," Bill claimed,
his head drooping. His knees began to tremble. "She
probably left them here," he claimed.

"Behind the books? You can do better than that,"
Greg challenged.

"Special Agent Parnell. We found this in the upstairs
bedroom," another one of the searchers declared, handing him a box. It was a shoebox for Timberland boots.
Greg looked at the sides.

"Size eleven and a half. Imagine that. Any boots to
go with this box?" Greg asked.

"No, sir," the deputy replied.

"Didn't think so. I suspect we already have them,
don't we, Mr. Meyers?"

"A DNA analysis should confirm it," Dan said. "If
you're not aware, Mr. Meyers, body sweat and hot feet
leave excellent evidence, even when you wear socks."

Bill Meyers gave a short, strangled cry, and his knees
began to buckle. The sheriff led him to sit next to his
wife. Crystal leaned her head against him and spoke
softly to him, stroking his hair.

It seemed to give him strength, because he sat upright after a minute. He looked at Dan and Greg with
renewed vigor before he spoke. "I would have lost
everything if that report came out," he said.

Crystal hushed him. "Save your strength," she urged.

"It almost worked out," he added.

"Yeah, you fooled us for a while. The boots you left in the truck nearly put Earl in prison or, worse, on death row," Greg said.

"Pretty clever, I must admit," Dan said, "leaving them behind to implicate Earl."

Bill Meyers smiled, and his chest shook. He began to laugh. "I wish I could take the credit. But to be honest, after I changed back into my shoes, I simply forgot them," he admitted. He laughed again, and a strange whistling sound emerged from his throat.

"We'd better go," the deputy remarked.

Bill stood and let the deputy escort him to a waiting cruiser.

Crystal followed but paused at the door to address Greg. "You haven't heard the last of us. We have very good lawyers, my husband and I," she remarked.

Greg waited until she was outside and then looked at Dan.

"You know, I hope that my marriage is as strong as theirs when I finally tie the knot," he remarked.

"Good grief. Can you imagine being married to a woman that cold and calculating? I'd be tempted to kill someone too," Dan joked.

"Cold and calculating, eh? So that would make her just like . . ."

"Don't say it. Just like every other woman on earth?" Dan asked.

"Well, not every woman," Greg admitted. "Just every one you've dated."

Dan laughed at the thought. "Perhaps a few, I admit." They headed into the driveway as the cruiser pulled away from the curb with Bill and Crystal Meyers in the back.

"Hungry?" Greg asked.

"I'm starving," Dan replied.

"I think Kelly's is still open. How's that sound?"

"Sounds good to me."

"Okay, I'll drive, you pay," Greg said.

Dan mumbled something unintelligible but followed Greg to his Toyota.

"So, when are you going to settle down?" Dan asked.

"What's the hurry?" Greg asked.

"Once you settle down, I can quit buying you dinner, and instead I'll come over for a home-cooked meal," Dan suggested.

Greg was silent for a moment.

"How's that sound?" Dan asked.

"Okay, my wife will cook," Greg conceded.

"All right."

"And you can stop at the grocery store for the food. I'll give you a list."

"Me? And what are you going to do?" Dan asked.

"Same thing I do now. I'll eat," Greg said.

Chapter Thirty

"It's beautiful here. What made you think of this place?" Amanda asked.

"Oh, a friend recommended it," Greg replied. "More Champagne?"

"Yes, thanks. It's quite romantic. You sure can pick 'em."

"I manage, somehow." He pointed as a great blue heron landed at the water's edge. "Looks like someone else came here for dinner too."

"Only he eats for free, right?" Amanda asked.

"He still has to work for his dinner. He'll sit there for hours, just waiting for his meal to swim past," Greg explained.

"The crab cakes were delicious," Amanda said with a smile. "If I had anything left on my plate, I'd offer him some."

"If you had any left, I'd take it," Greg joked.

She looked up at the sky, where the sun threatened to dip below the western horizon. Orange and pink colors hugged the tree line around them.

"Guess we should get going, huh?" she asked.

"If we're going to beat the dark, yes. Unless you'd like to stay. There's another world that comes to life after the sun goes down," Greg offered.

Amanda grimaced. "I don't think I'd like to spend the night out here," she said. Then she giggled. "Although I'm sure I'd be safe with you."

"Of course, Little Red Riding Hood," Greg teased.

They stood up. Amanda cleaned up their plates and plastic cups while Greg wiped out the pan and closed the portable campfire stove he had used to cook the crab cakes. When he finished, he swung his backpack over his shoulders and walked to the water's edge, where Amanda stood gazing over Lake Drummond.

"Do you bring all your dates here?" she asked him in a teasing tone.

"So far, every one."

"Really?" she said with surprise. "How many has that been?"

"Including you? One," Greg answered.

Amanda laughed, and they turned and began to walk up the Washington Ditch.

"So, tell me again the legend of The White Canoe," she said.

As Greg began to speak, he gestured with his right hand and shyly slipped the other hand into hers.